BAD
IDEAS

BAD IDEAS

A NOVEL
MISSY MARSTON

Editor for the press: Susan Renouf
Cover design and book illustrations: Tierra
Connor

Purchase the print edition
and receive the eBook free!
For details go to
ecwpress.com/eBook

Get the eBook free!*
*proof of purchase required

This is a work of fiction. Names, characters,
places, and incidents either are the product of
the author's imagination or are used fictitiously,
and any resemblance to actual persons, living or
dead, business establishments, events, or locales
is entirely coincidental.

LIBRARY AND ARCHIVES CANADA
CATALOGUING IN PUBLICATION

Marston, Missy, author
      Bad ideas : a novel / Missy Marston.

Issued in print and electronic formats.
ISBN 978-1-77041-461-7 (SOFTCOVER)
ISBN 978-1-77305-321-9 (PDF)
ISBN 978-1-77305-320-2 (EPUB)

I. TITLE.

PS8626.A7677B33 2019   C813'.6
C2018-905343-7   C2018-905344-5

The publication of *Bad Ideas* has been generously supported by the Canada Council for the Arts
which last year invested $153 million to bring the arts to Canadians throughout the country and
is funded in part by the Government of Canada. *Nous remercions le Conseil des arts du Canada
de son soutien. L'an dernier, le Conseil a investi 153 millions de dollars pour mettre de l'art dans la vie
des Canadiennes et des Canadiens de tout le pays. Ce livre est financé en partie par le gouvernement
du Canada.* We acknowledge the support of the Ontario Arts Council (OAC), an agency of the
Government of Ontario, which last year funded 1,737 individual artists and 1,095 organizations in
223 communities across Ontario for a total of $52.1 million. We also acknowledge the contribution of
the Government of Ontario through the Ontario Book Publishing Tax Credit, and through Ontario
Creates for the marketing of this book..

ONTARIO
CREATES

**ONTARIO ARTS COUNCIL
CONSEIL DES ARTS DE L'ONTARIO**
an Ontario government agency
un organisme du gouvernement de l'Ontario

**Canada Council
for the Arts**

**Conseil des Arts
du Canada**

Canadä

PRINTED AND BOUND IN CANADA

PRINTING: NORECOB   5   4   3   2   1

MIX
Paper from
responsible sources
FSC
www.fsc.org   FSC® C103560

For John & Cathy, Don & Dave

WHY DO THEY DO IT?

Why do they do it? What makes them drive their fists through walls, through windows, into each other's faces? What makes them press the burning ends of cigarettes into the backs of their hands while staring into each other's eyes? Why do they ride wild horses, bucking bulls, motorcycles, whatever crazy, dangerous, stupid thing they can climb onto? And when they are thrown, trampled, broken to pieces, what in God's name makes them get back on?

What makes a man imagine that he can drive a car up a ramp and fly over bales of hay, buses, creeks, canyons and forget that he will break his ankles, his ribs, puncture his lungs, bounce his brain off the inside of his cranium when he lands? If he is lucky. If his sorry life is spared one more time.

And why are these the ones? The ones making noise, wasting space. The ones that are covered in scars, that should be dead. The ones with less than half a brain inside their heads. Why are these the only ones she ever loves?

And here comes another one — sad story and all. His jeans riding so low, his T-shirt so thin, his eyes so dark. Jesus Christ. She's a goner.

Again.

PART 1

TRUDY

BECAUSE IT HAD BEEN YEARS

When those strangers walked into the Jubilee restaurant, Trudy Johnson was twenty-two years old and she had not had sex in five years. Her horniness was closing in on her every thought. It was making her edgy, irritable. But she had made herself a promise. She had decided to forgo the physical for a while. She was in recovery.

Trudy had the kind of body that caused no end of trouble. Her mother had the same one. Her sister Tammy had it. And her little niece, Mercy, would likely have it one day, too, God help her. The kind of body that grew up too soon, that alienated you from your later-blooming classmates. That attracted the attention of the wrong men. Or maybe it made men act wrong. It made them call you a goddess but treat you like trash. Impregnate you and evaporate. The Johnson family had, at this point, three generations of females living in their house and zero generations of men.

She had the kind of body that, if you lived in it long enough, confused you about love. It could lead you to believe that any man who really cared for you would not want to have sex with you. Because he would be able to see that sex was not your only purpose. That you had other things to offer. So far, she had not met such a man.

Except once, in a way.

Once she had met a man who was not the least bit interested in having sex with her. Maybe because he saw people naked every day, all bodies — even hers — had lost their magic. Dr. Noel Cameron had saved her life once. No questions asked. Every time she saw him in town, he nodded at her, then looked away. The sun always seemed to be behind him, shining all around his big head.

That was it: one shining exception to the rule. One good man. The rest, Trudy was pretty sure, were complete bastards.

BECAUSE THE AIR BECAME WATER

That first spring evening seemed like a long time ago now. A lot can happen in seven months. A lot can fall apart. Trudy would say that it was like a scene in a movie, except no movie she had ever seen was set anywhere that looked anything like Preston Mills, Ontario. Scrubby shit-town clinging to the bank of the cold grey St. Lawrence River.

Eight hundred inhabitants, one grocery store, one gas station, one corner store called Smitty's where you could fill tiny paper bags with stale penny candy. Swedish berries, toffee nuggets, black balls, licorice nibs.

One pool hall that no female would dare enter and that hollering, fighting men tumbled out of at hourly intervals each evening.

Six churches, one of them Catholic, one evangelical — complete with snake-handlers and speakers of tongues — and four barely distinguishable flavours of Protestantism: Presbyterian, United, Lutheran, Anglican.

A mile east of town, one massive set of locks that huge tankers eased into and then were slowly lowered and released to continue along the river to the ocean.

And there was a mill, WestMark Linen Mill, that employed Trudy and her mother, Claire, as well as most of the other working adults in the town.

There must have been other mills at some point, at least one other, to justify the town's name. Maybe a long time ago, when it was Preston Mills, the first. Because this was Preston Mills, the second. Preston Mills, the ugly.

In the 1950s, the town had been taken apart and reassembled between the river and the railroad tracks when the Seaway went through. Highway H2O, they called it. The way of the future. Higgledy-piggledy little Preston Mills — with its winding streets and courtyards, its barns and chicken coops and crooked lanes, its docks and boathouses and pebble beaches — was taken apart and put together again in straight lines. Houses jacked up, wrenched from their foundations, lifted onto trailers behind trucks, dragged back from the water, and deposited on dirt lots along a grid of new streets. Schools and churches were taken down brick by brick and built again. The scar of the old town was still there, at the bottom of the river: the streets, the sidewalks, the rectangular concrete foundations, the fence posts. A map-like outline of the whole town imprinted on the riverbed. And every day giant ships passed overhead, casting shadows over the sunken town like long black clouds.

Graveyards were moved, too. Coffins dug up and tombstones moved to flat treeless fields. People worried that the workers had lost track, that the bodies no longer matched the names on the stones. But how would they ever know? They wouldn't. The empty graves were flooded along with everything else. Slowly erased by silt and stones and shells and waving fields of seaweed.

(There were still bodies under there, though. Everyone knew it. For some of the dead, living relatives could not be found, and in the absence of a decision-maker, the bodies were left where they were. And some people were too squeamish or too superstitious to have their loved ones disturbed. Slabs of stone were placed over the graves to ensure the coffins didn't float up to the surface after the flood. A sad fleet of haunted little boats bobbing around here and there on the surface. Nobody wanted that.)

A new arrow-straight highway bordered Preston Mills to the north. The old highway was underwater about a hundred feet from the shore. In a couple of places, it rose out of the water and dipped back in, like the humps of the Loch Ness monster. Enough grass had broken through the asphalt and grown weedy-high that the hills looked like small islands. But if you swam out to one, you could see it was a road. There was a faded yellow line down the centre, and you could walk along until the road sloped back down underwater. In some places you could walk for half a mile before you lost your footing and started to float above the road.

That was how Trudy had felt when she first saw him: like the ground was suddenly dropping away beneath her feet, like the air had become water and she was floating up toward the bright blue sky.

BECAUSE THEY HAD NO RIGHT

It was April 1978. Mercy was only four years old and it seemed like the whole town had turned grey. The grey river washed against the grey shore. The grey trees stood against the grey sky, biding their time, refusing to bloom. Trudy and Mercy were sitting in a booth at the back of the Jubilee, and Mercy was peeling the cheese off her slice of pizza and cramming it into her mouth, her little hands covered in sauce. Trudy was smoking, staring past Mercy out the front window of the restaurant, when the door opened and the bells jingled. Two men came in, laughing so hard that they staggered and bumped against each other as they made their way past the front counter.

Both tall. Both lean.

Both dressed like they were from somewhere else. Lower, tighter jeans. T-shirts with dumb slogans.

I'm with Stupid. Keep on Truckin'.

One of the men was pale and freckled with curly dark hair and giant sideburns. The other man had broad shoulders and a broad smile. His skin was a deep, rich brown. This was a show-stopper. Every single one of the eight hundred inhabitants of Preston Mills was as white as paste — of English, Irish, Dutch, or German extraction — and not one of them had ever seen a black man except on TV.

"What?" said Mercy, seeing Trudy's eyebrows lift. "What are you looking at?"

Trudy scowled at her and shook her head, reached across and touched her finger to the little girl's lips. *Quiet.*

Mercy wrapped her hand around her aunt's finger and pulled it aside. She whispered, "Trudy, what?" Not waiting for an answer, she rose to her knees to look over the back of the booth.

"Sit down, Mercy." Trudy ground her cigarette out in the ashtray and took a sly look around at the other patrons. Nine or ten others, mostly men. Frozen. Staring. That giant fool, Jimmy Munro, pushed his chair back from the table, stood up, and lifted his chin at the strangers. He was always looking for a fight. Trudy could see him sizing up the newcomers, assessing his chances. Mercy brushed a fly off her forehead and looked from Jimmy to the strangers and back again. Jimmy said, "Can we help you with something?"

The freckled one pushed his hands deep into his front pockets, rocked back on the heels of his boots, and smiled. Trudy could see a good three inches of tanned skin between his belt and the bottom of his shirt. She could see the shadowy trail of dark hair down the middle. Like an oasis in the desert. Unable, or unwilling, to take her eyes off this welcome sight, she reached blindly across the table and tugged at the back of Mercy's shirt so that the little girl dropped back onto her seat.

"You know what?" said the stranger. "That's nice of you, but we're just here to see our friends." He caught Trudy's eye and nodded. Then he and his companion walked right over to their table and sat down.

As if it were true. As if they had any right.

"Thanks for letting us join you, ladies. Such a friendly little town."

Trudy knew she was being observed. Her feelings about this stranger were equal parts rage and attraction. And she was painfully tired. Her eyes were burning from cigarette smoke. She had a full night shift at the factory ahead of her and she had been chasing Mercy all day. And now she found herself in the middle of this ridiculous standoff.

"Listen," she said.

"Jules," he interrupted.

"What?"

"Jules Tremblay. That's my name. And this is James." James nodded. Trudy thought she would die of irritation.

"Listen, *Jewels*. And James. Nobody in this restaurant believes that you are my friends."

"Why not?"

Trudy sighed. "Because they all know me, and they know I don't have any friends."

"I'm your friend," said Mercy.

"Right," said Trudy. "I have one friend." She looked over at Jimmy and his table of galoots. Flipped her middle finger at them. They looked away. "Time to go, Mercy. Say goodbye."

"Bye, friends," said Mercy, quietly.

"You guys should probably go, too. Nothing good is going to happen here."

Trudy grabbed her jacket. The men stood to let them out of the booth. Mercy looked back at them and waved as Trudy dragged her to the front of the restaurant to pay.

And she knew it already. Trudy knew that even though it was indefensible, even though he had done nothing to distinguish himself, even though she knew nothing about him at all, she would think of him.

She would think of him and little else until she saw him again.

BECAUSE EVERYTHING STOPPED MAKING SENSE

Before he had shown up, bringing with him the tight green buds of springtime, things had been alright for Trudy. Boring, maybe. But alright. Mercy was hard work, especially when she was smaller. Pulling on Trudy's pant leg. Tearing the house apart like a little animal. Trailing chewed-up food and snot wherever she went. Still — it had been just the three of them, and things were simple. Trudy's mother, Claire, worked the early shift at the linen mill. Trudy worked the late one. They looked after Mercy in opposite shifts: Trudy on days, Claire on nights. At least, that's what they had done since Trudy's sister, Tammy, had fucked off into the ether and left her progeny behind.

Trudy spent hazy days on the couch, drifting in and out of sleep, TV on, one ear on alert for Mercy. Sometimes, out of nowhere, the little girl would bounce onto her, knocking the wind from her lungs, and then settle her warm little body behind Trudy's knees or in the curved hollow of her belly.

The nights passed in a blurry clockwork dream. Seated at her machine, fluorescent lights humming above, she sewed pillow-case after pillowcase. A straight seam up the left side, crank the wheel, sink the needle into the fabric, lift the foot, rotate ninety degrees. Lower the foot onto the fabric — pink or blue or green or some pastel paisley print — and sew a straight seam across the top. Needle in fabric, rotate ninety degrees, straight seam down the right side. Lift foot. Cut thread. Slide the pillowcase across the table into the bin.

Next.

One foot in front of the other, day after day, night after night. A carton of cigarettes, purchased each payday. A stack of packs, each cellophane wrapper unwound and discarded. Silver foil removed from one side then the other. Ashtrays filled and then emptied. Until he came along.

Then everything got complicated.

BECAUSE NEVER IS A LONG TIME

In a town like Preston Mills, people would say that a girl had "a reputation." There was only one kind. Trudy had known what this meant for as long as she could remember. Her mother had a reputation. And Trudy didn't want one. She had developed a defense. When adults asked if she had a boyfriend, she told them that she didn't like boys. They were disgusting. She almost believed it. By the time she was thirteen, adults stopped asking her about boys, and kids started calling her gay or a *lez* — Preston Mills–speak for lesbian. She let them believe it. Any boy permitted to touch her was usually from out of town (sports tournaments and visiting cousins provided the occasional make-out partner), sworn to secrecy, and threatened with death.

And she never, never went all the way.

This strategy had worked through most of her teens. Until Jimmy Munro finally wore her down.

Jimmy Munro's face looked like it had been hit with the back of a shovel: dented brow, crushed nose, chipped teeth. His dark eyes glittered with bad intent and he wore his hair Elvis Presley style: slick with Brylcreem and combed back over his ears. Trudy had known Jimmy since kindergarten. (She had known everyone since kindergarten.) In their first year of high school, he started hounding her. Sitting next to her in every class, goading her relentlessly.

"Hey, Trudy. You gay?"

"Shut up, Jimmy."

"What a waste. With that ass? Oh my God."

Trudy would stare straight ahead, trying to focus on the teacher.

"You don't know what you're missing, Trudy. I could show you something. You wanna see something?"

"Gross. Not interested."

He persisted.

Every class, every day, an endless stream of increasingly obscene banter. Until the words became meaningless. Until they stopped making her angry. Until there was something comforting about the tirelessness of his pursuit. It made her like him a little bit. Plus, he made her laugh. And hanging out with Jimmy — who was gigantic — deflected the advances of other boys.

Even when he was only fourteen or fifteen, Jimmy had been built like a bull. Thick broad shoulders and tiny ass. He was so top-heavy it seemed like you could tip him over with just a little nudge. But you couldn't. Trudy knew it. Sometimes when they were goofing around, she would throw herself at him in a wild tackle, to no avail. She would just rebound off him. He was as immovable as a mountain.

Then one day, walking home from school, she caught him off guard. She saw him walking down the path behind the Catholic church, about fifty feet ahead. She took a running leap at him at a slight angle and knocked him to the ground. *Whump!* She rolled on top of him, laughing. "Victory is mine!"

"Jesus, Trudy! You scared the shit out of me."

She leapt up, fist in the air. "The winner! Thank you. Thank you." She swept low, taking a deep bow.

He stood up and lunged after her, grabbed her from behind. He pressed his shovel face into her neck and whispered in her ear. "Trudy Johnson, will you never fuck me? Really? How can that be?"

"Never." Famous last words. "Now get off me."

BECAUSE SOMETIMES YOU CAN SEE THINGS
COMING FROM A LONG WAY AWAY

Trudy had quit school when she was sixteen to work at the mill. By the time Tammy was pregnant with Mercy, Trudy had already been working there for a year. One year that felt like forty. Every night that summer, she left early for work so she could go swimming. She would throw her bag over her arm and set out walking.

Ten at night and everything would be dead quiet. The sky was always black, the silver stars sparkling, the streets deserted. Almost all of the houses dark. The soft summer breeze smelled like the river.

She would walk right down the middle of the street, slowly, daring a car to come, daring the universe to break her perfect record: in the whole time she had been working at the factory, she had never once seen a car or a person on the street at this time of night. Straight ahead, up the hill, past the park, she could see the lights of the mill. But instead of going straight, she would turn left, cut through the school parking lot, across the baseball diamond, and down the gravel road to the beach. Each night of the summer, she would walk to the far end of the beach by the pier and the boathouses, place her folded towel on top of her bag, take off all her clothes, and walk into the water until it reached her neck. She would stand there, shivering a little in the black water, watching the moon's reflection on the surface until her heart slowed down.

A moment of cool peace between the heat and noise of home and the drone and glare of work.

She could see the lights of the factories across the river on the American side, and she could see the towering shadow of the hydro dam to the west.

One night, she stood there, about twenty feet from shore, her toes pressed into the silky clay of the riverbed, when she felt the rumble of a ship engine coming up through the ground. A green light flashed at the top of a buoy straight ahead. She heard the ship's horn and turned to the east to see the glimmer of it in the distance. She stood rooted as the ship took form, the vibration growing stronger, rattling her body. She was thinking about how long you can see things coming sometimes — sometimes for your whole life — when she turned and saw him standing on the shore.

Jimmy looked around, making sure nobody was nearby, and took off his shirt and then his pants. With the glow of the town behind him, he was just a shadow. But Trudy knew exactly who it was. She knew the shape of him. Looking at him standing there on the shore, she felt something brush against her ankle under the water. She kicked at it and took a few stumbling steps toward shore. She felt it again, slick and muscular. Higher on her leg now. Was it an eel? She lurched forward again, her bare breasts now well above the water line. The ship was right behind her now, easing past, stretching across the horizon. The ground was shuddering. He ran into the water, splashing, tripping forward, until he fell at her feet.

And that was it. The end of reason. Three years of firm resistance overcome by his hand on her knee under the water. His breath. The bubbles fluttering up her bare legs.

Once, she told him. And never again. And she really did think that she meant it.

BECAUSE EVERYONE MAKES MISTAKES

The Johnson house, rented from Trudy's grandparents, was so small as to be comical. A tiny cube covered with fake-brick asphalt siding, topped with a pitched roof. The ground floor housed the kitchen and the front room that doubled as Claire's bedroom. (Every morning, she removed the sheets and tucked them into the side table, folded the hide-a-bed mattress back into the couch.) Stacked on top were the bedroom shared by Trudy and Tammy — and later, Mercy — and the closet-sized bathroom. Shag carpet in every room. Wallpaper, too. Wood-grain wallpaper, floral wallpaper, even (in the bathroom) fairy wallpaper. A birch forest mural featuring a waterfall on the back wall of the front room.

Small, carpeted, wallpapered to death and stiflingly hot.

By the end of that summer, when sixteen-year-old Tammy was eight months pregnant, Trudy thought the house was feeling even smaller than usual. She also felt that her sister was using her condition as an excuse to take liberties. She had decided to draw a line.

"Why are you such a bitch, Trudy? Just get me some ginger ale. I'm thirsty."

"I said, get it yourself. You're pregnant, not crippled." The smell of cabbage rolls was fumigating the house. Claire had been crying and furiously cooking for months. Ever since Tammy's pregnancy had become undeniable. Claire had been a mother at seventeen and now she would be a grandmother at thirty-four. She was beside herself with shame and worry. Frenzied. The freezer was as packed with casseroles as Tammy was with child. Trudy felt like she was going to vomit. Why was this house always so disgustingly hot?

"You've always hated me. Always thought you were better than me. Some big sister you are."

Trudy stood up, her body suddenly beyond her command, a machine carrying out its simple unstoppable function. She walked over and pushed the heel of her hand against Tammy's chest, pinning her against the couch. She could feel Tammy's heart beating, her clammy skin sweating under her hand. "What did you say to me?"

"Get off! *Mom!*"

"Girls?" Claire's nervous voice from the kitchen.

Trudy straddled her sister, a knee on either side of her thighs on the couch, pushed her hand harder into Tammy's chest, feeling the slight give of the sternum. Why was she doing this? Her breath was shaking. "Shut up, Tammy. Why don't you ever think of anyone but yourself? God, you're right. I do hate you sometimes."

Trudy pushed herself off the couch and turned away. The thick funk of cooked cabbage filled her throat. She bolted up the stairs.

Retching into the toilet, the idea spread through her like a stain.

Biggest mistake of her life.

Fucking Jimmy Munro. Of course.

BECAUSE IT WOULD KILL HER MOTHER

"Trudy, are you OK? Let me in."

"Leave me alone, Tammy."

Tammy sat in the hallway with her back against the bathroom door, her giant belly pressing the air out of her lungs, forcing her to sit up as straight as possible just so she could take a breath. "Oh my God. Are you pregnant, Trudy?"

The door opened suddenly, throwing Tammy off balance. She almost toppled over. "Get in here. Don't say that. Do you want to kill our mother?"

"Well, are you?" Tammy sat on the edge of the tub. "It wouldn't be the end of the world, you know. We could raise our kids together! *Happy families.*" She said this last part in a loopy singsong voice.

Psycho, thought Trudy. She put her toothbrush in the dirty mug by the sink and turned to her sister. "Tammy, you have to have sex to get pregnant. You know I don't do that."

"Yeah, right."

"I'm just sick. I need to see the doctor."

BECAUSE SMALL TOWNS ARE UNBEARABLE

Trudy's hand was shaking so that the receiver of the telephone vibrated against her right ear. She had dragged the phone as far into the bedroom as the cord would allow. She sat on the carpet between the twin beds and spoke quietly with her hand cupped around the mouthpiece.

"And what is it concerning, Trudy?" Dr. Cameron's nurse waited for a response. This nurse was named Janet McElroy. She used to babysit Trudy and Tammy when they were kids. She still lived right across the street. Small towns. Unbearable.

"It's private."

"You know we keep things confidential here, Trudy. I need to tell him something. That's just how it works." Trudy didn't believe it for a minute. She had heard enough stories to know *how it worked*. So-and-so had cancer. And Mrs. So-and-so had warts on her behind. Baby So-and-so got dropped on his head. She knew who she was talking to: Radio Free Preston Mills.

"It's about my period. It never stops." This was in the right neighbourhood. But the opposite of the truth. She wrote her appointment time on the inside of her wrist with a blue ballpoint pen. Just numbers and symbols. Like a secret code: 3:00280873.

Three days, two hours, ten minutes into the future.

BECAUSE ENOUGH WAS ENOUGH

Trudy told Jimmy enough was enough, they were never supposed to have done it in the first place, and now it had to stop. Though, of course, she didn't tell him why.

"No problem," said Jimmy. A little too quickly, Trudy thought. "Yeah, right."

"No, really, it's OK. I got a girlfriend now anyway."

Trudy checked to see if she cared about this. She thought she didn't, really. At least not very much. "Good."

"Are you mad at me?"

"Nah." And she wasn't. She was mad at herself, the universe, her mother, her stupid sister. But not Jimmy. She just couldn't see why she had risked so much for so little. Why her body had taken over her mind like that. Well, that was done with now. Brain back in the driver's seat, please.

"Hey, Jimmy."

"Yeah?"

"Go fuck yourself."

"Yeah, yeah. You're tough, Trudy."

"Don't you forget it."

Tough. (Except there was a breach in the system, a leak, a pressure valve in the form of a small round bald spot at her crown.

Trudy had been pulling out her hair. She would stare off into space, twist some strands around her index finger, then run the hair through her fingers, letting it fall away until a single strand remained pinched between thumb and forefinger. And then with a quick tug she would pull it out and brush it off her hand and onto the floor. By the time she went to see Dr. Cameron, there was a quarter-sized patch of soft scalp showing. Sometimes she wore a kerchief to cover it. Other times she carefully teased her hair, blasted it with hairspray, and patted it carefully into place over the spot. Nobody would ever know.)

Tough. (Except she had terrifying nightmares. Earthquakes bringing down the house around them. Or floods. Water rushing through the house, sweeping away hairbrushes, slippers, packs of cigarettes on the crest of a giant wave. Or snakes. Snakes oozing up out of the ground in the yard, slithering through open windows, under the doors, rippling through the carpet, wrapping around her ankles. She would wake up kicking and tearing at the sheets, Tammy staring at her in the dark from the other side of the room.)

BECAUSE SOME SOLUTIONS CAN FIX
MORE THAN ONE KIND OF PROBLEM

Dr. Cameron told her to get dressed and he would be back in a minute. Miserable, Trudy swung her legs over the side of the examination table and hopped down, her bare ass hanging out of the gown, lubricant making her thighs slippery. Oh, she felt low. She grabbed some tissues from the box on the desk and cleaned up and then she took a few more and blew her nose. Not sure what else to do, she put the used tissues on the crinkly paper on the table, covered them with her gown, and got dressed. She sat on the black vinyl chair in the corner, shivering in her jeans and T-shirt, dreading whatever would come next.

She was thinking about Tammy, about how wrong it seemed that she became prettier and happier with each week of pregnancy. Her face was rosy and full, her hair thick and glossy. Her breasts and belly were firm and round and perfect. Laughing and smiling all the time. As if she didn't have a care in the world. As if she had no idea what could possibly be wrong with being sixteen years old, single, unemployed, and pregnant. Trudy, on the other hand, was feeling tired and ugly and hollowed out. Nauseated and conquered.

Dr. Cameron knocked once as he opened the door. He was already in the room by the time Trudy had even noticed the sound.

"Trudy, here's what we're going to do. There is a very easy way to address this problem. I'm assuming it's a problem, Trudy?"

She stared at the doctor for a moment, not sure she understood.

"Trudy, there is an operation that we do sometimes, when girls' periods are too heavy. I think it would be a good idea for you. Essentially, we just put you to sleep and scrape the lining of your uterus. It sort of just gives you a fresh start."

"But, I haven't had my period in months."

Dr. Cameron sighed and looked down at his hands in his lap. "Trudy, this procedure works for all kinds of problems, and I think it might be the best thing for what's bothering you. But you tell me. What do you want to do?"

Gratitude made her weak, made her body limp. "I want the operation. Thank you, Dr. Cameron."

On the day of Trudy's procedure, Tammy drove her to the hospital in Harristown, half an hour away. The sisters held hands across the bench seat the whole way there and said nothing. Trudy looked out the window so she didn't have to look at Tammy's belly almost touching the steering wheel.

Two weeks after her surgery, Trudy had a follow-up appointment with Dr. Cameron, where she sat through his gentle — and embarrassing — speech about preventing unwanted pregnancies. As if she didn't know. As if she hadn't learned her lesson. She left the clinic with a year's supply of birth control pills in her purse. Free. Just in case, he said. You'll have them if you need them. Ninety-nine percent effectiveness rate, he told her.

But she knew a way that was one hundred percent effective. It had worked for her in the past and it would work again.

Zero access. Closed for business. She put the pills in the top drawer of her dresser, buried beneath underpants and nightgowns.

Until five years later when Jules Tremblay walked into the Jubilee restaurant.

BECAUSE YOU CAN'T HELP LOOKING

Trudy wondered how things had turned out at the Jubilee that night. If there had been a fight, surely people would be talking about it, but she had heard nothing. She thought that likely Jules and James had taken her advice and left quietly. Maybe they had simply gone back to wherever it was they had come from.

Then, a few weeks later, there was a sighting.

She had been walking from the grocery store to her car, a bag balanced on one hip, Mercy holding her hand.

"Trudy." Mercy came to a dead stop and pointed across the parking lot. "Trudy, your friends are here!" Mercy's tiny, bony fingers dug into her wrist as she worked to pry her hand out of Trudy's grasp.

"Mercy, stop! You're hurting me. You stay right here. There are cars." She looked up, and sure enough, there was James walking toward them with yet another stranger. As if once they began there would be no end of strangers just appearing in Preston Mills. This new stranger had floppy blond hair and pale blue eyes. He looked nothing like Jules Tremblay. Except for the sideburns. It seemed to Trudy that a person could identify any man not from Preston Mills by his sideburns. James shot a twinkly smile at Mercy.

"Mercy, my friend! How are you?"

"Fine."

"You really are fine." He said, making Mercy giggle. "And how is this fine lady?"

"Trudy? She's fine!" Mercy shouted. Trudy said nothing, shifted the groceries to her other hip.

"This is my friend, Mark. He's visiting from the wild west."

"Is he a cowboy?"

"Absolutely! You see that belt buckle?" Trudy couldn't help it. She let her eyes drop to the silver belt buckle gleaming in the sunlight. "That's from a real rodeo."

"Mercy, come on. Let's go." Trudy pulled on Mercy's hand until she sort of toppled toward her.

"Bye!" said Mercy.

As they walked away, James yelled after them, "Trudy! Jules would love to see you!"

Trudy kept walking, dragging Mercy along.

"I'll tell him you say hello!"

Trudy was blushing and sweating as she fumbled with her keys, trying not to drop the groceries as she unlocked the car. Mercy was bouncing straight up and down as if she were on a pogo stick. "Trudy, you have so many friends now!"

BECAUSE THE BLACK WATER
WANTED TO SWALLOW YOU WHOLE

Her car. How Trudy loved her car! A nine-year-old Dodge Dart purchased from a high school friend who owned a body shop out on the highway north of town. Two-door, dark green with black vinyl seats and a horn that worked about half the time. She had saved her money for five years to buy it. It was not that she loved it as an object, especially. But she loved the feeling it gave her. False to be sure, but it gave her the feeling that she was the master of her own destiny.

Often, she would go for a drive after dinner, turn the radio on, and, if it was warm enough, crank the windows all the way down. She would open the giant ashtray, big as a dresser drawer, and push the lighter in. To Trudy's amazement, the car had come equipped with a dash-top cigarette dispenser. It was a small black leather box with silver trim and a button on the front left. She could just hit it and a cigarette would pop up like a little soldier, filter end up. Amazing.

After the grocery store and their encounter with James and the cowboy, Trudy dropped Mercy off at home. She pulled into the driveway, put the car in park, and, with the engine running, reached across Mercy and opened the passenger door. "Out you go. Grandma'll make you dinner."

"Aren't you coming, Trudy?"

"Nope. You go in, sweetie. I'm going for a drive."

"What about the groceries?"

"I'll bring them in later. You go. *Out! Shoo!* See you later."

Trudy watched Mercy run to the side door and bang on it with both fists. The door opened, Claire leaned out and waved, and Mercy disappeared inside.

Trudy backed out of the laneway, eager to be away. She headed east, out of town, turned onto River Road, and followed what was left of the old highway along the river. The road dipped and curved. At certain points it came alarmingly close to the water, tilting the car on a sharp angle. As if the road wanted to tip you into the river. As if the river wanted to swallow you whole. No guardrails. Just the water, black and rippling on the right, almost level with the road.

And farms, apple orchards, houses, shacks on the left.

Coming around a sharp curve, past the Riverside Campground — which was more trailer park than campground — Trudy hit the brakes, almost colliding with a giant bulldozer inching its way across the road. She put the car in park and waited for the machine to cross. She looked over at the field on the left and was stumped by what she saw. What used to be a grassy pasture was covered with earth. Piles and piles, tons and tons of dark brown earth. Mountains. Trudy tried to guess what might be going on. It could, she supposed, have something to do with shipping. A new pier? Whatever it was going to be, it was ugly now. She put her foot down and pulled around the back of the bulldozer. Clouds had crowded over the sun and the sky was as grey as metal once again.

Trudy drove away, past the graveyard, up the hill to the parking lot at the Point. She pulled up to the chain-link fence facing the lock, shut off the engine, and lit a cigarette. Turned on the radio. "Big Yellow Taxi." God, she hated Joni Mitchell. There was something so phony about her, so shamelessly girly. Too much *feeling*. It set Trudy's teeth on edge. She turned the radio off and rolled the window down. The air was mild and damp. The breeze rippled through the grass on the hill leading down to the narrow channel of the lock. The deep groan of a ship's horn sounded to the west. She could see the ship in the distance, rust-red and black. She got out of the car and leaned against the fence, forearms resting on top. The sun broke out of the clouds as the giant bow of the ship nosed into the channel. From where she stood, it looked as if there were only inches between the side of the ship and the cement wall of the lock.

The boat was as long as a football field. And tall. The men on deck looked like ants. Out of habit, she waved. They waved back. She had been doing this her whole life. She and Tammy had stood at this very fence as little girls, ice cream cones in hand, sticky ice cream dripping onto their fists, waving high above their heads, hoping the sailors would wave back. And they always did.

The ship inched along through the cement channel, passing Trudy by. The black lettering on the rusted hull said UNDAUNTED. Each letter as tall as a man. She watched the stern move slowly away, the water churning white behind it.

BECAUSE THE LIGHT AT SUNSET
CAN MAKE ANYTHING LOOK GOLDEN

The sun was setting as Trudy pulled back onto River Road, red and orange and shining right into her eyes. She pulled down the visor and leaned against the door, trying to find an angle that wasn't blinding. She wanted to drive back past the construction site at Robson's farm for another look. The sky was darkening behind her as she pulled over to the side of the road by the field. Across the road, the river was pink with the reflection of the sun. The sunset made the piles of dirt look different now: metallic and golden. The yellow tractors and bulldozers were still, scattered across the field, as if all the operators had been vaporized mid-shift.

Headlights from behind lit up the inside of her car, getting brighter as the car approached. But instead of going past, it veered off onto the shoulder of the road, coming straight at her. Trudy braced for impact, but the car came to a halt just inches from her back bumper, spraying gravel into the air. She sat frozen as the lights went out and the engine sputtered to a stop. She heard the thump of the driver door closing, the crunch of boots on gravel coming toward her, but she was too frightened to turn around. Suddenly the golden light turned grey. The sun had gone out. And Jules Tremblay leaned into her passenger window, smiling that smile.

"What do you think?"

"I think you're an asshole. You scared the shit out of me."

"I mean, what do you think of my little project?"

Jules opened the door and slid into the passenger seat.

"You see that island over there?" He moved over beside her and pointed past her face out the driver-side window at the river.

Trudy saw the long, narrow island covered in brown grass about halfway across. She could feel the heat coming off him, his chest almost touching her back. "Yeah, I see it."

"We're building a ramp in that field, and I'm gonna drive a rocket car off the end of it and land on that island."

"A rocket car."

"That's right." Jules pulled his wallet out of his back pocket and produced a folded-up newspaper clipping. It was faded and limp with wear. There was a picture of what looked like a Cadillac with a turbine strapped to the trunk and strange, stubby little wings attached to its doors. The headline read, "Crazy Canuck to Jump St. Lawrence in Rocket Car." The car in the picture was a fake, he explained. Cobbled together for promotion. Tinfoil and glue and fireworks. The real rocket car was being built in Chicago. It would cost a hundred thousand dollars.

One hundred thousand dollars.

"You're not serious."

"Oh, I'm serious. I've got investors. Even got a TV deal."

"You're crazy."

Jules shrugged and looked out the window. "Yeah, maybe."

They sat there for a while — Jules looking out at the piles of dirt, Trudy looking at the island — not knowing what to say next. Jules opened the passenger door and got out. He turned back and put his head through the window again.

"Was that your kid?"

"What?"

"Back at the restaurant. That little girl. Is she yours?"

"No. She's my sister's. Why?"

"Just wondering."

"Well, now you know."

"You should come visit us some time. Me and James. We're out on Old Murphy Road, right before the tracks. Bring the kid if you want." And he turned away. She watched him in the rear-view mirror, walking back to his car. He nodded at her as he opened the door and got in. The engine made a loud, deep rumble. He backed up at top speed, then roared past her and cranked the wheel, spinning the car around in a full circle, leaving a black doughnut of rubber on the road. The rear end of the car dangled off the edge of the road, tipping toward the riverbank for a second, before the wheels caught the turf and the car sped away.

Idiot, she thought. *Crazy, stupid idiot.*

With dark brown eyes. And eyelashes like a girl.

Christ.

BECAUSE SOMETIMES YOU HAVE
TO SET THE WORLD ON FIRE

Back at the factory for another shift, Trudy found herself thinking about her father and how little she knew about him. She knew that his first name was Darren, but her mother refused to tell her his last name. She never understood why Claire protected him, why she wasn't furious about being left alone with two kids. Trudy struggled to understand why, in fact, Claire still pined for him two decades later. "I'd have him back," she would say, with that soft look on her face. That soft, crumbling, injured expression that was on her face most of the time. It was infuriating.

Trudy was pushing pillowcases through the machine, dropping them into the bin in a trance. She wondered what Darren was doing now, if he had kids with his actual wife. If they all got up every morning, went to school and work, came home and had dinner together in complete ignorance of his other offspring. She wondered if these imaginary kids were somehow better than Tammy and her. If they were finishing high school, playing sports, saving themselves for marriage or whatever. Probably. She wondered if it could possibly be true that Darren had loved Claire. That, as Claire claimed, he had loved Trudy and Tammy but had to do the right thing and go home. Coward.

He was a coward, and her mother was, too. Trudy would have followed him home, toddlers in tow.

Or so she thought.

She liked to think of herself as tough, as a trailblazer, but maybe she was just a pushover like Claire. Look at her now, taking care of Tammy's kid, working nights in the same shitty factory as her mother and every other loser in this town. It wasn't as if she was setting the world on fire.

An empty serger spool hit Trudy in the back of the head and she flinched, pulling the pillowcase she was sewing to the side, the seam veering off the edge of the fabric. "Look alive, Johnson!" Trudy turned around to see Jeannie Burns leaning back in her chair, laughing along with the other hyenas in the fluorescent light of the sewing room. "You think you're good, don't you, Trudy?"

Here we go, thought Trudy. How was it possible for someone with absolutely nothing to do with your life to have such strong feelings about you? It had always been this way. Since they were little kids. Jeannie hated Trudy. Was it jealousy or just sport? Who knew? But it was time to shut it down. "Shut up, Jeannie."

The other women turned back to their machines. Pretended to focus on their work.

"Not sure why you think you're so great, Trudy. Slut for a mother, slut for a sister."

Trudy lifted the foot on her machine, pulled the pillowcase out and cut the threads, reached for the seam ripper, and started to tear the seam out.

"You pretend to be so pure, Trudy, too stuck-up for guys around here. But I heard otherwise. I heard Jimmy Munro had you under the bleachers when you were fourteen. Said he couldn't fight you off."

"In his dreams."

"More like a nightmare, if you ask me. He said you were like an *octopus*, hands everywhere. So desperate."

Trudy threw the botched pillowcase on the floor. She got up from her chair and walked toward Jeannie's station, not sure what she was going to do when she got there. Though Jeannie looked startled, she got up from her chair and braced herself. She stood tall, pressing her fists against her thighs. But Trudy could see them trembling. The radio, turned to the usual American station, was playing "Da Doo Ron Ron" by The Crystals. Trudy grabbed Jeannie's wrist and twisted her arm behind her back. She put her other hand on her throat, pushed her thumb and forefinger into either side of her neck.

"You're right, I *am* like a fucking octopus, Jeannie. See? And what are you like?" Trudy drove her knee into the back of Jeannie's knees, so that she collapsed forward onto the ground, kneeling. "What are you like, Jeannie? Tell me." Trudy was kneeling behind her on the hard cement floor, twisting her arm just a little further behind her back before releasing her. Shoving her forward onto the ground. "Nothing. That's what you are." Trudy dusted herself off and walked back to her machine. "And tell that fucking retard, Jimmy, to keep his mouth shut."

Trudy's hands shook as she fed another pillowcase into the machine and lowered the needle into the fabric. The air vibrated around her.

Da-doo-ron-ron-ron, Da-doo-ron-ron.

BECAUSE NOT EVERYTHING HAS TO MAKE SENSE

"Wanna go for a drive, Mercy?"

"Sure!"

"Alright. Go get your kangaroo jacket. But don't tell Grandma, OK?"

"OK!" Mercy tore up the stairs to get her jacket and returned, struggling to put it on. "Why can't I tell Grandma?"

"Because if you tell her, I won't take you again." Trudy spun Mercy around so she was facing away, pulled the sleeves of the jacket right side out and pulled Mercy's hands through, then spun her back around and zipped her up.

"Why's it called a kangaroo jacket, Trudy?"

"Guess."

"Because it makes you feel like hopping!" Mercy hopped around the living room with her hood up and hands in her pockets.

"Try again."

After a few seconds: "Because it has pockets like a kangaroo!"

"Bingo."

"But kangaroos only have one pocket, Trudy. My jacket has two."

"That's true. Not everything has to make perfect sense, you know. Kangaroos have pockets, the jacket has pockets. Close enough. Come on, let's go."

"OK." Mercy bent deep at the knees and hopped through the kitchen toward the back door. Trudy grabbed her keys off the rack and followed her out to the driveway. You didn't have to spend much time with little kids to realize that they were not so different from dogs: sometimes the best thing, the only thing, was just to get them outside and let them run around until they wore themselves out.

BECAUSE NOT ALL UNICORNS HAVE HORNS

"Can you put my window down, Trudy?"

"Sure, babe. Just for a minute. It's chilly out there."

"Where are we going?"

"Maybe we can go to the park at the Point. You can go on the swings."

"Yeah!" Mercy was on her knees on the passenger seat, her head and shoulders leaning out into the wind. "Hooray!"

Trudy reached over and tugged her back into the car by the back of her jacket. "But first I want to drive down Old Murphy Road."

"No! That's boring, Trudy. I want to go to *the park*!"

Trudy said nothing, just turned on the radio, signalled left, and pulled off the highway onto Farley Road and then onto Old Murphy. Glum, Mercy slumped down in her seat and watched the trees go by. Trudy slowed down as trees gave way to pasture and pavement turned to gravel. "Baby, look! Horses!"

"No. I'm not looking."

"Mercy, these are the prettiest horses I've ever seen." She pulled the car over to the side of the road. "Come on."

Trudy killed the engine and opened her door. Mercy got out, too, staring at her feet as she went but clearly warming to the adventure. Trudy helped her across the ditch, lifting her over the water rushing at the bottom, and they made their way toward the field. Leaning against the log fence, they could see the horses in the distance. Two of them, white as snow, the sun lighting them up like lanterns against the blue sky and green grass. Mercy sighed, her cheeks pink from the cool spring air. "Trudy, I think those are unicorns!"

Trudy laughed. "I don't know, sweetie. They don't have any horns."

"That's just because they're too young. Those are unicorns. UNICORNS! COME HERE!"

One of the horses lifted its head and stared. Mercy squeezed Trudy's hand and stood perfectly still. "I think they're coming over," she whispered. "Stand still."

Both horses were staring now. One of them threw its head back and whinnied. The other nodded and both of them started to walk toward the fence. Mercy was twitching, fidgeting, trying to control the urge to jump up and down. "OK, unicorns," she whispered. "Just a little bit closer."

The horses kept coming and Trudy started to get nervous. She had never been very close to a horse before and could not quite believe the size of them as they approached the fence. She took two steps back, taking Mercy with her. The horses pressed their chests against the fence and leaned their heads down toward them. Trudy could feel their hot breath. Their nostrils flared. Mercy took a small, careful step toward the fence. One horse took a step back but the other leaned closer. She reached her small hand out and ran it down over the horse's nose.

Trudy was holding her breath.

The horse leaned down and nuzzled Mercy's kangaroo pockets, nudging her belly, knocking her back a step. Mercy held her hands above her head as though the horse was a bandit and this was a holdup. The horse snorted, backed up, turned, and walked away. The other followed. Trudy let her breath out. "Jesus!"

Back in the car, Mercy said, "That was a unicorn, Trudy. I could tell. His nose was so soft."

Right before the railroad tracks on Old Murphy Road, down a long dirt lane, was an old red-brick farmhouse sinking into the swampy earth beside a shallow bay thick with rushes at the shore. A car was parked in the front yard, and tire tracks made muddy trenches in the grass. A sprawling willow tree leaned into the water. Trudy took her foot off the gas and glided past the lane. A plywood sign hung from a post. JULES TREMBLAY HEADQUARTERS spray-painted red in stencilled letters. She pulled over onto the shoulder and killed the engine, looking at the house in the rear-view mirror. Mercy climbed over the front seat and tumbled into the back to look out the back window. "Who lives there, Trudy?"

"Nobody." They sat for a few minutes in silence.

"What if my mom lives there?"

"That would be a surprise."

"Trudy, I miss my mom sometimes."

"I know, hon."

Trudy caught sight of Jules's old Pontiac GTO coming up behind them, turning into the laneway. Flat black, it looked like someone had painted it with house paint and a roller. Probably rusted to dust under there. Likely paint was the only thing holding it together. Edgy, she started the car and pulled out, heading for the highway. "Let's go to the park, pal."

"I don't want to go to the park anymore. I want to go home."

Trudy looked at her niece in the rear-view mirror. Curled up with her arms crossed, her chin pressed into her chest, her knees drawn up. There were acres of car seat around her. She was a tiny little thing. Just a speck.

"Or we could visit some friends. What would you think of that?" Trudy slowed down, looking for a place to turn around.

"What friends?" Suspicious but hopeful, Mercy sat up in her seat.

"Our new friends, remember?" Trudy pulled into a lane between two cornfields, came to an abrupt stop, and backed out heading back the way they came.

"Cowboys!" shouted Mercy.

"Sure. Cowboys," said Trudy.

And she headed back to HQ.

CLAIRE

BECAUSE YOU CAN'T JUST LAY DOWN AND DIE

Trudy was right. It was true that Claire wasn't angry at Darren, that she daydreamed every day about his return. About how he would walk through the door and tell her he had been wrong to leave, that he hadn't been happy for a second without her, that wild horses could not drag him away again. And she would tell him that she had done her best with the girls, that he had a granddaughter. She would tell him that she had waited, that she had been true. That no man had touched her since the day he left. Not one. Not once.

(Not that anyone cared to believe this. There was no redemption in Preston Mills. The evidence was clear: two children with a married man by the time she was eighteen, her own daughter pregnant at sixteen. She had been a bad girl and now she was a bad mother. Her own parents barely spoke to her. Unless the rent was due. She had the sad life she deserved. End of story.)

Oh, and wouldn't they all be surprised! Her parents, her daughters, everyone at the factory. The busybodies at the coffee shop. How surprised they would be to see that tall strong man on her arm! They would see the way the girls had his eyes and not her own. Those clear blue eyes. Claire didn't believe for a minute that Darren loved his wife, that he had other children. It was not possible. It did not square with the dream she dreamed. And without that dream, what did she have? If she dared to look at the world without that rosy tint, what would she see?

A tiny house.

A gruelling job.

A missing daughter.

An empty bank account.

An old flannelette sheet and a shabby moth-eaten blanket pulled out of an end table every night. A thirty-nine-year-old woman with blond hair and black roots, sleeping alone on a lumpy hide-a-bed. Unloved, disrespected, alone. In a town made of mud and gravel and weeds. Inhabited by bullies and gossips. Brutes and harpies.

That's what.

So she kept her eye on the prize. Inside Claire's head was a running narrative, telling her story. The story of a princess abandoned and forgotten, mistaken for a scullery maid, biding her time, awaiting the return of her prince. Her patience would be rewarded. Those who doubted her were to be forgiven for taking her at face value, for believing that she was only what she seemed.

But she knew better. She was the star of this movie. And it would have a happy ending.

Otherwise, she might as well just give up. She might as well just lie down on the dirty kitchen floor and die.

BECAUSE IT WASN'T CALLED
"THE NUMBER TWO" FOR NOTHING

Claire always had a flair for fantasy. It had not gone unnoticed. It began with a pair of shoes. In 1955 in Preston Mills, ladies' shoes were available in black, brown, and — in the summertime — white. The only way to get shoes of any other colour was to go downtown to Mackenzie's Dry Cleaners and order a pair of cloth bridesmaid's shoes. Plain white satin pumps that could be dyed any colour to match any dress. When she was sixteen, the year she met Darren, Claire had saved up enough money, cut a tiny piece of cotton from the hem of her favourite dress so she could match the colour precisely, and ordered her shoes. Size 7, narrow. Candy-floss pink. Then she waited six weeks for them to arrive.

She had also gone down to Jameson's Pharmacy and purchased a half-dozen packets of Dylon Intense Rose fabric dye and spent her evenings during that spring dying all of her white blouses and sweaters, white socks, white brassieres and underpants a bright, vivid, rosy pink. She dyed her brown hair Miss Clairol Shade Number 129: Butter Cream Blonde. And when she walked down the street, it was as though she left a trail of fairy dust behind her. Or sugar. Men couldn't take their eyes off her. Her figure like the number eight, her fluffy blond hair, her flushed

48

cheeks and black lashes, her pink sweater, pink dress, pink shoes. Her pink chiffon scarf knotted at her throat. She was like sexy, walking candy.

Being sexy candy, Claire made enemies of most of the girls in Preston Mills. They shook their heads, fake-coughed into their hands, saying, *Whore!* as she walked by. They spread outrageous rumours about her. That she had sex in the bathroom of the gas station or behind the bar at the legion hall. That she had a third nipple, a second vagina. Or no vagina at all. Herpes. Scabies. Warts. They would say anything to taint the fantasies their boyfriends were surely having about her.

Not that those girls had ever liked her anyway, had ever trusted her. It seemed to Claire that not even her parents had ever really liked her. *Yeah? Well, fuck them!* That's what Claire's only friend, Nancy Meyers, said. *Fuck'em if they can't take a joke.* At eighteen, Nancy had seemed so much older than Claire, so much more at ease in the world. They had made friends on a smoke break outside the mill one day. Nancy had moved to Preston Mills from Brockville to get a job and to be closer to Jason MacNeill, the fuck-up. The dick-weed. A short-lived romance, Nancy would call it. The bloom was off *that* rose in short order. But who cared? Nancy Meyers said that it was raining men in Cornwall. Just a half-hour drive away, there were tens of thousands of new men, working men, from across Canada. Even from the States.

Those men were going to dig canals, build new roads, dam the river, and flood almost every shitty little town along Highway 2, including Preston Mills.

Good riddance!

They didn't call that highway "The Number Two" for nothing. That cowpat-spotted, pothole-covered, thistle-lined highway. Bring it on, giggled Nancy and Claire. Buh-bye, Preston Mills!

BECAUSE LOVE AT FIRST SIGHT IS REAL

That first night at the Pioneer Hotel in Cornwall, Claire saw him standing alone at the end of the bar. Tall, strong, sandy-haired, and sad-looking. Stubble on his chin, a cigarette tucked behind his ear. The pack rolled into the sleeve of his white T-shirt. The filthiest fingernails she had ever seen. That gold ring gleaming against the brown skin of the ring finger of his left hand. He looked up and smiled tightly, shyly. She saw it, the idea of her, passing across his face. The blond girl with the pink shoes and her big, mean-eyed friend, parking themselves at the bar as if they were old enough to drink. He drained his glass and walked away. Out the door to the parking lot, into his truck before she could catch his eye one more time.

Before she could smile that smile again.

And just like it was in every corny movie she had ever seen, the sight of him had filled her up with fantasies of a new life. She thought she had seen her future when she saw that man at the bar. (Years later, in that shoebox house back in Preston Mills, tears would fill her eyes when she thought of it. How strong and pure her hope had been. How fully and simply she had expected a grown man to come into her life and take her away from this place. How she had expected to become something better.

But Darren Robertson was no prince.

He was hardly even a man. He was just a boy, transplanted from some other sad small town not much different from her own.)

Claire followed him out to the parking lot as though she were in a dream, as though the normal rules of life had been suspended. As though love at first sight were real. He looked at her through the windshield and shook his head. *No way.* He shooed her away with his hand, as you would a dog. She turned around and walked slowly back across the parking lot to the bar, her pink heels sinking into the soft mud, the street lights shining down on her like a spotlight. He would be back the next night. And she would be waiting for him, her Butter Cream hair perfectly teased and sprayed, her pink sweater straining across her chest.

And her heart bursting with fervent, crushing teenage love.

BECAUSE THERE WAS NO STOPPING IT

Claire had met Darren Robertson in April. By June, she was pregnant.

But to tell it that way, to lay out these few bare facts — he was married and away from home, she was a small-town girl with a bad reputation, they met in a bar, she got pregnant — to tell it like this, was wrong. These facts lead you to obvious conclusions: that she was easy, that he was callous and irresponsible, that her pregnancy was a tragedy. None of this was true. To get to the truth of it, the truth that her daughters would never believe, you had to tell the story right. You had to try to explain the feelings you had when you did the wrong things.

First, for example, people might be surprised to find out that in spite of her hair and wardrobe, her knockout body, Claire had been a virgin when she met Darren. In Preston Mills, boys had kept their distance. They hated and feared her. The propaganda campaign executed by the local girls had worked exactly as planned. The only person Claire had ever kissed was her friend Nancy, "for practice."

Second, Darren loved her. This was a fact. And he loved her more than he loved his wife. Here is how she could tell: every word, every laugh, every kiss, every beautiful thing between them made him sadder. And every stupid thing about her made him love her more. When she finally wore him down, after they had finally kissed in the front seat of his truck, he had put his hand on her shoulder, held her at arm's length, and hung his head like a sad old dog. He looked up to heaven like a suffering saint. And then he sighed and leaned in for more.

When he finally took her to his trailer and unbuttoned her blouse and pushed her skirt up her legs, he laughed when he saw her home-dyed pink bra and panties and, later, when he saw the faint pink shadowy outline of her on his white sheets, the smudge of Dylon Rose. But after they finally did it, after they finally took off all their clothes and pressed their naked bodies together, after he slowly, carefully pushed his way inside her and they both felt like they would die of terror and relief, when it was all over and they lay breathing heavily into each other's necks, he cried like a baby. He cried because, like her, he felt lost, hopeless, and wrong. In love.

And there was no stopping it.

BECAUSE YOU CAN DEFINITELY
MAKE THE SAME MISTAKE TWICE

You might think that Darren and Claire were hoping for the best as they had sex over and over again at the height of their young blossoming fertility, or that they were blind to the probable consequence of their incessant coupling. But you would be wrong. They knew Claire would likely get pregnant, and, unreasonably, they had wished for it. They wished for a baby. Because this wish was somehow, in the haze of 1950s' romance, inseparable from their love. Because the force of it was irresistible.

And they knew there would be no making it right. But being right was not what mattered. What mattered was the thrilling, doomed, happy-miserable, love-drugged dream they were living. What mattered was the way collapsing into each other's arms blotted out all the pain and worry and daily harassment of their lives.

And you might think that Claire would make this mistake only once. This terrible miscalculation that landed her back in her furious parents' house, begging to be allowed to keep her baby, promising she would be a good mother if they would just help her. But you would be wrong again. She would make it twice. For Tammy and Trudy were full-blooded sisters, born of the one great love of Claire's life.

Love of my life, thought Claire, staring out the kitchen window. Words. Words that always seemed corny unless it was you. Unless it was you saying these things to the person you love. The person who made you feel like your heart was being crushed. These embarrassing things they said to each other, Darren and Claire, that they meant *with all of their hearts*. The things they would say again and again. *Like they were under a spell.* They were all true.

I love you.

I have never loved anyone like I love you.

I will never love anyone this way again.

Nothing else matters.

Never leave me.

Think of me always.

You are everything to me.

I am nothing without you.

Nothing.

She had not, of course, thought any of it through. She had only been helpless against it. And so after he had gone, she found herself stranded in Preston Mills, even lower on the social food chain than she had been before, facing condemnation everywhere she went, struggling to be something she had no idea how to be: a mother.

Darren, of course, had returned regularly to his wife in New Brunswick for visits and, eventually, for good.

He could see no other way.

The last time he saw his daughters was on Tammy's second birthday. Trudy had been three. At Claire's instruction, she called him Uncle Dee.

Kiss your Uncle Dee goodbye, Trudy. He has to go.

Tammy told Claire she didn't remember Darren. She didn't remember standing, holding hands with her mother and her sister, watching his truck kick up dust as it pulled away and raced down the road, as it became smaller and smaller, until it disappeared over the horizon. She didn't remember how long the little girls stood at the end of the driveway, terrified and confused, waiting for their mother to stop crying.

But Trudy remembered. She said so. Back when she used to talk more. When she was less angry about everything.

Trudy said that she remembered the rough scrape of his stubbly cheek against hers. She had never seen a man cry before and there were tears leaking out of the corners of his eyes as he held her little face in both of his hands. She remembered that he smelled like laundry smelled when it came in from the line. He smelled like the blue sky.

Like the thin air he was disappearing into, thought Claire.

BECAUSE MEMORIES ARE MORE
IMPORTANT THAN REMEMBERING

Claire knew she had it wrong. But this was the way she remembered it. The workers and everybody else had called it "Inundation Day," the day the dams were blown up and the water flooded the old towns. She had never heard that word before. Inundation. It made her think of a spell. An incantation. A word that could change one thing into another. Which, of course, it did.

Inundation Day. And also Dominion Day: July 1st. Thirty tons of dynamite, blowing the stone cofferdams to smithereens. Smithereens. Another word to marvel at, to roll around her mouth like hard candy. They only came with explosions, those smithereens.

But, man, when they came it was magic.

A shower of stone, clouds of smoke like spirits rising, and a torrent of water. A towering wall of water washing it all away. Rolling over the fields, the lanes, the old stone canals. The empty square foundations that snaked along the winding roads of her childhood: erased.

(It wasn't really like that, Claire knew. There was a blast and a wall of water, but the flooding of the town was more gradual. A sort of slow seeping out, taking days to fill the new channel. But Claire liked to remember it like Niagara Falls thundering down Main Street.)

Her parents' small house had been uprooted, trucked across town, and deposited onto a new foundation in the middle of a mud lot on a new street, too close to their neighbour's house. No grass. No trees. But a gravel driveway and a brand-new mailbox. And a view out the back window of mud, rubble, and sky. There was an ugly strip mall on the highway and a gas station. And they were close enough to the mill to walk to work.

The only green grass was in the graveyard. All the stones were arranged in neat rows in chronological order, with their mismatched bodies under the ground or no bodies underneath at all. Just stones on top of blankets of fresh sod on top of dirt. Just stones in a field of green, green grass.

She knows it is wrong, but in her mind it all happened on the same day.

The day the Seaway was flooded and all the men were done work. The day her parents' house was moved onto its new lot. The day the Queen of England came through on her own giant boat. And the day Tammy was born. There were fireworks on all those days, she swears. There were fireworks and tears. Joy and pain. The beginning and the end. All at once. Inundation.

What she remembers is this.

The deafening explosion.

Darren's hand in hers. Rough and dry and warm.

The shrapnel of stone scattering in the air like fireworks in the brilliant blue sky.

The wall of water rushing, tumbling forward. The earth rumbling beneath their feet. The fields, the streets, the sidewalks disappearing under the waves.

The heat of the July sun. The cold mist coming off the water.

The heat of the water rushing out of her, soaking her feet. Her pink shoes. The skin on her legs wet and cooling in the summer breeze.

The pain in the bottom of her belly like fireworks.

The house in the middle of the mud lot. The Royal Yacht Britannia gliding by so close to the shore it seemed like you could reach out and touch it.

The fireworks. The parade. "O Canada."

The waving green grass in the field full of stones.

The hot blanketed bundle of the baby in her arms. The sweat of her brow. The salty sweetness of his kiss.

The incantation.

Don't go. Don't go. Don't go.

BECAUSE HATE CAN BE LOVE

But on some level, Claire knew. She knew which year was which. Which bright hot July 1st brought the breaking of the dam ('58), which one brought the Queen in her boat ('59), and which one brought that little bundle of trouble she had named Tammy ('57). But it all melted together in the blinding sunlight shimmering on the water. In the heat-wave warp of love.

Oh love, love. Where have you gone? Where have you ever been? Up in the big blue sky above the clouds. Or somewhere down deep beneath the waves. Razed and flooded. Drowned and blotted out.

Except for those few short years of brilliant sunshine with Darren.

Love! There was never enough love. Not for Claire. So hungry for love from the beginning, her mother used to push her away with a broom.

The summer Tammy was born, Claire remembers being cooped up in her parents' house for days, her belly so heavy, so stuck out in front of her she almost fell forward every time she stood up. Her feet were so swollen, none of her shoes fit. Only her slippers. The heat was making her miserable. One-year-old Trudy was miserable, too.

One day, Claire remembers, Trudy had been fussing all day. Pouting and crying. Refusing to eat. Then, finally, she was sleeping, her head tucked hotly into Claire's neck. The shoulder of her blouse was wet with drool and sweat. Trudy's little body was pasted against her. Claire had put her head back on the arm of the couch to close her eyes, hoping to sleep just for a minute, when her mother walked into the living room. Hair slick with sweat, face bright red, broom in hand. She looked at her daughter and her granddaughter with pure scorn.

"I can see you're very busy, Claire, but that diaper pail upstairs is disgusting. Could you please do something about it?"

"Yes," Claire whispered. Trudy stirred in her arms, whimpering. "Today?"

"Mom, I will get to it. Please keep your voice down. I just got her to sleep." She gingerly — and with much effort — got up from the couch to take Trudy to her crib in the corner of the room. Trudy's eyelids twitched and her brow furrowed for a moment as Claire set her down and quietly backed away. Suddenly angry, she turned to her mother. "You could be a little nicer to me, you know." And then, "Sometimes it's like you don't even love me at all."

As Claire brushed by on her way upstairs to face the nauseating diaper pail, her mother's hand shot out and grabbed her. Her strong fingers dug into Claire's plump, tender upper arm. Her mother's face was in her face. Her voice trembled.

"Listen to me, you little idiot."

Claire listened.

"I have cooked for you, cleaned for you, let you live here in my house, when the whole town is looking down their noses at me. When the whole world knows I have a daughter who can't keep her legs together. Who has no sense. Who refuses to learn from her mistakes and comes back to this house pregnant again! *Twice!* Single and pregnant again and barely eighteen! Brilliant." She paused here. Shook her head in disgust and loosened her grip on Claire's arm. "Don't you ever fucking tell me that I don't love you. You stupid, stupid girl."

Claire's slipper caught on the edge of the rug and she stumbled forward a little toward the stairs, tears streaming down her face, her arm burning where her mother had grabbed it. Those words, spoken with hatred. Spat at her like venom.

Don't you ever fucking tell me I don't love you. You stupid, stupid girl.

That was as close as her mother had ever come to saying it.

BECAUSE THE SADNESS CAN JUST START LEAKING OUT OF YOU

Claire liked to look on the bright side. It was in her nature. And in spite of her mother's gloom, her dire warnings, Claire thought that her life had turned out OK. She had Trudy, steadfast and true. Not uncomplaining, nobody could accuse her of that, but solid as a rock. Tammy, on the other hand, was bad. There was no denying it. Bratty, volatile, lazy. But when Mercy was born, Claire thought it might all have been worth it. That beautiful baby.

But she knew. They all knew almost right away. Tammy would not be a mother to that child. It was so sad to witness that Claire was almost relieved when Tammy left. She was ashamed to think it, but it was true. A new peace descended on the household. Order was restored. Claire and Trudy settled into a rhythm and Mercy settled down and it all felt like it could work.

Then one day, about a year after Tammy's departure, something happened. Claire lost sight of the bright side. It all closed in on her. She missed Tammy. She worried about Mercy. And Trudy. She felt all of their lives were heading in the wrong direction and that it was probably all her fault. Her mother had been right. She was useless. And she was so very lonely.

So this deep sadness had been awakened in her. A genie she could never quite get back in the bottle. It just lurked in her heart all day every day, barely suppressed, until a moment came when she was too tired to hold it in. It was happening now. Claire had been crying for days and days. For weeks. Unable to stem the flow. As she leaned over her machine at the factory, tears would drip off her chin and onto the fabric. Her nose ran constantly, causing her to sniffle.

"Allergies!" she would say brightly to anyone looking her way. "Just allergies!" Of course, it was nothing of the kind.

Lying in bed at night, she felt a pinch in her heart. A sharp, physical, painful pinch. "*Oh!*" she would cry. "*Ouch!*"

And the unfairness of it — that she should have physical pain heaped on top of her sadness — made the tears start again. And then the crying made her lungs hurt. It was as if she were being punished for being sad.

One night, her arrival heralded by the flip flop of her slippers, Mercy stood at the foot of Claire's bed, looking at her grandmother, squinting into the dark. "You OK, Grandma?"

"Sure, sweetie. I'm OK. Just a cramp in Grandma's big ugly foot."

Mercy giggled but still stared. "Are you crying?"

"No, baby. My eyes are just leaky. I'm tired. Go back to bed, hon."

Mercy gave a sleepy little wave and turned around and walked back up the stairs, her slippers slapping her heels. So Claire found a way to stop making sounds when she cried, and the pain moved down from her chest into her stomach and pinched her there. And the tears just leaked and leaked out of her eyes all night and all day and all night again.

For days and days and days.

And then she met Speckles the Dog.

BECAUSE MAMA NEEDS LOVE

Claire's old friend, Nancy Meyers, had been after her for weeks
to come see the puppies, but she had said no. They couldn't possibly have a dog. Didn't they already have enough to do, enough
to take care of, she and Trudy? And then on the twenty-third
day of crying, when she felt that her sick stomach was sloshing
around full of saltwater, when she couldn't take it another minute,
she had started thinking wistfully about puppies. How one might
sit on your lap so that you could stroke its head or scratch its
back while you watched television. How a puppy might sleep at
the foot of your bed, how it might lick your salty old face in the
morning to wake you up. How it might get you out of the house
and walking around the neighbourhood, talking to people. And
what a nice companion a puppy might be for Mercy!

And so on.

So she said to her friend Nancy, OK, she would come over
and look at them, but she wasn't making any promises. She was
not taking one home.

Nancy had answered the door in a stained house dress, her
hair a mess, the powerful smell of dog coming off her, and a tired
half smile on her face. She made Claire squeeze through the door,
opening it only wide enough to get her body through so that the

dogs would not bolt. Wet muzzles were pushing against Claire's ankles, and she was laughing before she was even fully inside the house.

As Claire waded through the dogs and sat on the couch, they swarmed her. Or tried to swarm her. She counted six puppies comically trying to heave their heavy bodies onto the couch and flopping back down onto the carpet. They were so big! Twice as long as they were tall. Their fur smooth and silky like velvet. They were snuffling and snorting and whining. "What kind of dogs are they, anyway?" She raised her voice to be heard over the racket. "They're such *big* puppies!" She couldn't stop laughing. She felt so happy.

A little weak, a little lightheaded, but happy.

Some of the puppies wagged their tails so hard they lost their balance and rolled onto their sides. Claire reached down to rub a soft belly.

"Basset hounds!" yelled Nancy from the kitchen. "Or part basset hound, anyway. Maybe German shepherd, too."

Then, with great effort, one of the huge puppies finally struggled up onto the couch beside Claire. It laid its head on her lap. The weight was unbelievable. Claire scratched the dog behind its big floppy ears and then rubbed its back. It sighed. A real human-sounding sigh. Its brothers and sisters whined at Claire's feet. As she worked her way down the dog's back, scratching, the dog grumbled, "*Uhr-ruhr-ruhr-ruhr.*"

"What's that?" asked Claire, leaning down and looking into the dog's eyes.

And she swears this is true.

As she scratched the dog's soft baggy hide, it said in a low grumbly whine, "*I love my ma-ma.*" Claire barked with laughter, and the dog howled to join in. The pinching feeling in her stomach disappeared. The match was made.

Speckles was coming home with Mama.

BECAUSE YOU NEVER GET A MOMENT TO YOURSELF

Claire was standing in front of the bathroom mirror. She puffed her pale blond hair with both hands and turned to look at her profile. She was still pretty, still passable. But her black sweater was pilling. It was covered with dog hair. There was even, Christ, a smear of dog drool or dog snot on her shoulder. *Jesus.* What had happened to her? She put toothpaste on her toothbrush and stared into her own eyes as she cleaned her teeth. She spit into the sink, rinsed. Claire took another look. She smiled and raised her eyebrows.

God. This sweater.

She pulled the sweater over her head and dropped it onto the floor. She fussed with her hair again and took another look. Her beige bra was greying. When had she started wearing beige bras? A nun would wear this bra. She decided to take the bra off, too, and stepped back from the mirror.

Ah. That was more like it.

She was smiling at herself now, turning to the side and winking at the mirror. Her figure was still good. For this, Claire was grateful. After both babies, she had had a few months of soft pillowy pudginess, and then it all just seemed to snap back into place like a rubber band. The magic of youth, she supposed.

Nature's wonder, Darren used to say.

She pushed her breasts together, leaned forward. Let her head fall back, pretending to laugh.

Hey, lady, you look good! the mirror seemed to say. *Well, thanks!* thought Claire. Thanks very much. She felt so much better. Dazzling, really.

"Mom?" There was a knock on the door. "Are you going to be long?"

Claire jumped back from the door a little and let out a yelp.

"Just a minute, hon. Almost done." She bent over and picked her bra up off the dirty floor. She was breathing heavily.

"I have to go to work soon, you know."

"I know, *I know*. Just a sec." Claire was sweating, so the elastic of the bra caught painfully on her skin as she tried to spin it around and get her arms through the straps. Trudy knocked again. "I know, I know!" Claire pulled her nasty, besmirched sweater over her head. Her hair was a mess. It looked like a crooked wig. Two seconds ago she was Marilyn Monroe. Now she was Phyllis Diller.

Except Phyllis Diller wouldn't be caught dead in this terrible sweater.

She opened the door, walked past her disgruntled daughter, and went downstairs to make up the couch for bed. Speckles, who had been sleeping in the hallway, got up and lumbered down the stairs behind her.

DARREN

BECAUSE TROUBLE WILL FIND YOU

Beer in hand, sitting on the step of the trailer he shared with three other Seaway workers, Darren stared at the moon and the moon stared back. A bright eye hovering over the water, asking him when he was going home and what did he think he was doing? And who for the love of God was that girl? What had he done?

On April 1, 1956, the day Trudy was born, her father, Darren Robertson, had thought, *God help her. She is beautiful.* So small, so perfect. His first baby. And not with his wife.

Said wife, Michelle, was not only childless but also — for the time being — husbandless. Back in Brownsville, New Brunswick, staying with her parents. Waiting for him to return with enough money to get their own place, maybe have some kids, to start a life. He said he had to go where the work was. Twenty thousand men were needed, and they would take anyone who could swing a hammer or drive a truck. The project was ridiculous. Whole villages would be flooded, displacing thousands of people. There were dams to build and miles upon miles of channels to dig. The giant St. Lawrence River would be backed up, diverted, then let loose. Washing the old towns away. New roads, new towns would be built.

It could go on for years, this project. *It could*, Darren thought, *go on forever*.

Of course, there were jobs back in Brownsville, or at least close enough to Brownsville to allow him to stay where he belonged. The truth was that he had run away, scared to death, feeling like nobody should count on him for anything. He had run far away, but somehow he had managed to create exactly what he had been running from. It was as if it had followed him here: adulthood.

Little Michelle. Only five feet tall, nineteen years old. But cranky as hell. Bossy. Mean, sometimes. She had held on to him so tightly the morning he left, he couldn't draw a full breath. Crushing him. Wetly snuffling into his chest. He had walked out to his truck in the freezing cold early morning air, resisting the impulse to run, to skip and jump, to speed away, his foot to the floor. This was true. Though, he did love her — in a protective, rough-and-tumble, bickering kind of way. And it scared him. He was only twenty-one, had only ever been fifty miles from home. He had believed that he was going away to find himself, to be among men, to settle down enough to settle down.

He hadn't gone looking for trouble.

But trouble found him alright.

Gorgeous trouble, half-drunk and teetering on cheap pink high heels.

BECAUSE EVERYTHING INSIDE
YOU HAS BEEN REARRANGED

Darren knew something about love. He knew that if you neglected it for too long, it could be erased. And that one love could replace another. Blot it out completely. His wife knew it, too.

That morning, so long ago, when he had driven away from Claire and Trudy and Tammy, he turned the radio up loud and cranked the rear-view mirror to the side so that all he could see, all that was reflected there, was the grey-blue river and the pale sky and not that sad trio standing at the end of the driveway, fading into the distance. And when he pulled into that other driveway back in Brownsville, when he put the truck in park and turned off the engine, he couldn't get out.

He sat there, staring at the front of his in-laws' house, at the yellowing cream polyester sheers pulled across the living room window, wondering how he could arrange his face so that nobody would know. How he could possibly convince anyone that he was happy to be home.

When his head, his chest felt hollow. When everything inside him had been rearranged.

Minutes passed. He saw the sheers part and fall back into place. Still, he couldn't move. He just sat there until the front door opened and Michelle came out onto the front step and stood there, hands on hips. Darren took a deep breath and opened the door, hopped down onto the gravel. His knees buckled. He steadied himself against the side of the truck and raised a hand to wave, pulled his face into a smile. He grabbed his duffle bag from behind the seat, slammed the door, and as he made his way around the front of the truck, he laid his hand on the warm metal of the hood, doubled over, and started to retch.

As his hot vomit splashed over the gravel and onto his work boots, Michelle turned her back on him and went into the house. And when she slammed the front door, her eyes turned from soft brown to flint.

BECAUSE YOU DON'T GET TO CHOOSE YOUR DREAMS

But he did go inside the house, finally. And he stayed. Darren stayed with Michelle and made the best of it, as they say.

And in twenty years away from Cornwall, Preston Mills, and the Seaway, Darren had never once dreamed about Claire. The only dreams he ever had about that time were about the tunnels and the fish.

At Long Sault, tunnels had been dug under the Cornwall canal so workers could get to the work site: a dam that would be thousands of feet long when it was finished. The Americans had built a pontoon bridge for their workers, but the Canadians hiked through tunnels under the canal like moles in the dark, emerging at the site dirty and clammy and blinking into the bright sunlight.

Ships were still using the old canal, and some mornings when Darren and the other men were making their way through the dark, damp tunnels, the earth would start to tremble beneath their feet and pebbles would tumble off the walls and onto the ground. They would stop, picturing the long ship passing overhead and praying that the walls would not fall in and crush them. Sometimes, he would wake in his bed, feeling the weight of the earth on his chest, the mud in his eyes.

And the fish. He had dreams about the fish. Two dams had been built a couple of miles apart, and the water between them pumped out over the course of weeks. When the bottom of the river was finally in sight, it was covered with fish and eels, flopping around in the mud. Darren and the other workers waded through them in rubber boots, carrying tubs of water between them and picking out the game fish to be returned to the river. The other fish, the "coarse" fish, would be shipped out, processed, and sold. Maybe they made cat food with it or something; Darren had no idea. They had been given charts to study. Good fish and bad fish. Pike, trout, bass, sturgeon: these were the good ones. He had tried to commit them to memory, the pictures of the green and silver and spotted fish, the placement of their fins, the shapes of their heads. He thought he was ready. But Darren had been stunned by the size and strength of some of the fish. Muskie, carp longer than your arm, weighing fifty pounds or more. Days and days he spent wading through the mud, the panicked fish flailing at his feet, thrashing in his arms, soaking his clothes, their powerful tails whipping around and bruising his thighs.

In his dreams, his boot catches in the mud and he pitches forward, falling hard onto the muddy, writhing riverbed. His body is sinking and the fish are flopping onto him, all over him. An eel slithers out of the mud and around his neck, the head of a huge carp thuds against the middle of his back, knocking the air out of him.

Michelle's flint eyes stared at him in the dark as he tore at the sheets, gasping for breath.

JULES

BECAUSE IT'S HARD TO TELL THE DIFFERENCE BETWEEN FLYING AND FALLING

Jules was about to fly. He was in the middle of an outdoor arena in upstate New York doing doughnuts in a beat-up piece-of-shit car, the wheels throwing up clouds of grey-brown dust. A couple of girls in cowboy boots and bikinis were walking around, holding up checkered flags as if this were a race. As if there were more than one fool in more than one car. He wouldn't be breaking any records today, not in this thing. An old hard-top convertible, the roof bolted on. He and the boys had removed the windshield (carefully — the scrapyard wanted to keep it), the side mirrors, and the sun visors. Anything that could come undone had been undone. He wished he had a better car, one with less rattle and give, but what the hell. Typical.

He had been touring for ten years with the International Hell Drivers. International because he was Canadian and the rest of the stunt drivers were from the States. He had been making about three jumps a week. Depending on the weather, his injuries, the ability to get shitty cars, to book dates in shitty towns. But now it was all about the Challenger. The pretend rocket car before the real rocket car. Now, it was all about promotion.

And then one last flying leap across the St. Lawrence River.

Jules took a final lap around the arena and turned sharp, fish-tailing into starting position. Dirt coated his teeth, his tongue, was caught in his eyelashes. He revved the engine and waved at the crowd. Maybe two hundred people scattered here and there in the bleachers. He took a few deep breaths of the warm June air before snapping his visor down. Sweat trickled down his back. The hair on his arms stood on end. *Watch this, fuckers.*

The film of dust on his visor made the world look dreamier, softer. The red, white, and blue paint on the ramp straight ahead was faded and blurred. The junkyard cars were lined up, numbers spray-painted on their hoods, one through sixteen. There was no ramp at the other end. He would land where he landed — likely on numbers twelve, thirteen, and fourteen.

The crowd was chanting. JUMP! JUMP! JUMP! He cocked his right knee back to his chin and drove it down onto the accelerator, laid his head back against the headrest. The car vibrated, rattled over the packed dirt, and made a hollow boom as the tires hit the wooden ramp. The steering wheel was almost shaking out of his hands, and, with a sickening falling away, a familiar lightness in his chest, he was airborne. Rising in a long arc up into the air, he looked out over the bleachers at the woolly clouds gathering in the blue sky; time stretched and stopped, letting him hang there and enjoy himself for a moment.

Like being at the top of a Ferris wheel, looking out over the fairground.

He shot a hand out the window in a quick salute, and the crowd went wild. He felt a slight tilt, a shift in the angle, and he grabbed the wheel again as if it would make any difference. As if he could steer with the wheels hanging helpless in the air. Blue, green, brown, white, grey, the cars passed below him, blurring together. He had a chance of a clean landing on the far side. Could he possibly make it? He leaned his chest toward the dash, trying to urge the car forward with his weight. The crowd was silent, rapt, breath collectively held.

The earth loomed as the car lost altitude. He came down hard on top of the last two cars, and his body pitched forward. Jules felt a jolt up his right leg. The car listed to the side, leaning off the edge of the heap of crushed metal. The crew ran across the field toward the car. His foot was still on the accelerator. Why? He pulled his leg back, but it was as if it were made out of mud.

The engine sputtered and died.

He looked down. His right foot was pointed slightly upward, toes toward him, and he couldn't straighten it out. He felt his boot tighten dangerously.

Something was broken. Again.

Shit–damn–fuck.

Christ.

Overtaken, defeated, he sat back and waited for the crew to come and help him out of the car. Rain began to fall. He could hear it. Raindrops on the hood, making bright spots in the grime. People in the bleachers stood and turned away, inching down the rows to the stairs. Jules reached down and unzipped his boot, pulling at the heel. His foot looked bloated and boneless in his dirty sock and pain rushed in, amplifying with every beat of his heart. Thump, thump, thump. He was sweating through every pore.

"The mic! Bring me to the microphone! Tell them not to go!" he gestured frantically as they pulled him from the car, waving his hand in a summoning motion, as if he could pull the microphone through the air toward him. The MC sprinted to the centre of the arena, grabbed the mic, and started talking fast, trying to get the crowd to sit tight. *Hold on folks. The Crazy Canuck has something to say.* The crowd waited. Mostly, they were still standing, half-turned away. The rain was getting heavier. This had better be good.

They carried Jules across the dirt in a stretcher, helmet still on, pushing his head awkwardly forward, his chin against his chest. At Jules's urging, one of the other hell riders raced over to the Challenger, parked at the edge of the arena, and revved the engine. Sparks and orange flames shot out of the turbine. People sat down. Put newspapers or jackets over their heads.

"That's my baby!" said Jules into the mic. "A lot of you probably know we're building a ramp in Preston Mills, on the Canadian side, and I'm gonna try to jump one mile over the St. Lawrence River in a rocket car. This summer. Stay tuned. Thanks for coming, folks! Now I have to go to the hospital." *Ha, ha,* thought Jules. *Very funny.* That punchline was starting to wear thin.

The crowd, what was left of it, clapped politely, gave a whoop or two.

The "rocket car" powered down with a chug and a clunk.

BECAUSE EVERYTHING LOOKS LEFT BEHIND

Jules drove back to Preston Mills left-footed, his right foot in a cast. Crutches leaning against the passenger seat. He crossed the border at Cornwall, the bridge arching high over the enormous St. Lawrence River. Dark and rough and rippling with menace. Some days, to Jules, it looked like it was teeming with monsters, masses of tentacles unfurling, waving just below the surface. The metal grate of the bridge made a hum against his tires. On the Canadian side, he pulled up to the customs window and handed the officer his birth certificate.

"How long were you in the United States, sir?

"Twelve hours."

"And what was the purpose of your visit?"

Jules offered a mumbling summary of events. "I'm a professional daredevil," delivered with a smirk. Sheepish.

"I see." The border guard looked down into the car at the crutches and the cast. "Room for improvement, I guess."

"Absolutely right." Jules nodded. "Yes, sir."

"On your way, then. Welcome home, Mr. Tremblay. Drive carefully." A wide smile broke through the guard's tough-guy demeanor as Jules pulled away.

Ridiculous. He felt ridiculous. Maybe he should have mentioned his TV deal, his future jump across the river, his big plans. But who would believe him, the shape he was in? Bags under his eyes, unshaven, slumped into the driver's seat in a filthy sweatshirt. His bare toes sticking out of the cast looked purple, suffocated. Pathetic. He turned onto the old highway to drive along the water, the road winding along beside marshy inlets and the old stone canals. Farm houses set far back in the fields down long lanes lined with scraggly wind-blown poplars. Grassy ditches flowing with muddy water. A dog here and there chained to a spike in the ground. Cows huddled together in pastures.

What a sad, magic place this was.

Every single thing looked unloved, forgotten, left behind.

BECAUSE IN THE COUNTRY, BIRDS MAKE AN UNBELIEVABLE RACKET

As the pavement turned to gravel on Old Murphy Road, he saw her car, the green Dodge, parked by the side of the road a hundred yards past the laneway. The little girl's face appeared in the rear window, a white circle. Jules thought he saw her small hand wave at him as the car pulled back onto the road and Trudy started to drive away. *Fine*, he thought. *Christ*. He turned into what passed for a driveway — really just a couple of muddy, pebbly tracks overgrown with tall grass — and he felt his tires sink slightly into the spongey turf.

He turned off the car and looked out at the bay, the cattails waving, rustling in the breeze.

A red-winged blackbird perched on a bending reed made a mechanical trill.

A kingfisher stood on the sagging hydro wire slung between the house and the pole at the road, its head turned sharply to one side.

Chickadees flitted about the bushes, and Jules sat in the car, listening to the birds and the breeze, trying to muster the energy to hobble and hop to the house and tell his stupid story.

The screen door opened and James stepped out onto the porch, smiling and waving him in. *Alright*, thought Jules. *Gimme twenty minutes, I'll be right there.*

Witnessing his elaborate tussle with the car door and the crutches, James and Mark came to his rescue, bearing him across the muddy lawn and into the house.

Finally seated at the round white Formica table in the middle of the old dilapidated kitchen, he was laying out his tale for the entertainment of his friends. The slate-coloured sky, the arena, the bikini-clad girls, the crowd (he doubled it in the telling, four hundred, maybe five), his approach, his mid-flight wave to the crowd. The height of his jump, almost over-shooting the landing (another lie), the moment of confusion when he realized his foot was still on the accelerator.

The crowd springing to its feet. (This was true, though their reason for standing was not fully explored in this version of the story.) His struggle to get his boot off before it was so tight it had to be cut off at the hospital, the pain. He was about to describe how they carried him to the microphone so he could address the crowd when suddenly he felt he was losing his audience, their eyes drifting to a spot above and behind his head.

His voice trailed off as he turned in his chair to see them through the screen door: Trudy and Mercy. There they were. The blackbird trilled and the rushes swayed at the shore of the bay. The warm late-afternoon sun was strong behind them, so that they were only shadows. Dark silhouettes brightly haloed by the glittering light.

BECAUSE YOU CAN ONLY DO
SOME THINGS FOR SO LONG

It took him just a beat too long to say something, to invite them in.

"You said we should come, so we came." She was belligerent, gorgeous. And he was so tired.

The truth was that Jules had had enough. He suffered. Lord, he suffered. He had broken so many bones so many times, he could barely get out of bed in the morning. Sometimes he could actually hear his joints creaking.

Pain, humiliation, brushes with death. No fame and not much glory.

Once he had been making a jump at a town fair, and he had run out of gas on the take-off ramp. That's how broke he had been. The car tipped off the end of the ramp and fell heavily onto the cars below with an inglorious metallic crunch.

Once he sped off a ramp, and somehow the car rolled in the air, landing on its roof on the ground. The car had crumpled like tinfoil around him. He was trapped. Sitting there helpless, losing consciousness, he could smell gas.

Then, he heard someone suggest using a torch to cut him out of the car.

This will be it, he thought, *killed by stupid ideas heaped on top of stupid ideas.* He had been very surprised to wake up alive and only slightly damaged. They had managed to pull him out without blowing him to pieces. He still had dreams about it sometimes: the smell of gas, the voices, the rasp of the lighter.

A few more car rallies and county fairs and then one massive jump. If he made it, he would be set: talk shows, merchandise, maybe even movies. If he didn't make it, well, his worries would still be over.

Because if he didn't make it, he really wouldn't make it. That much seemed obvious.

Mark told Mercy and Trudy to sit down, and he went to the fridge. One ginger ale, one beer. Jules saw Trudy eyeing his cast. "I'm almost thirty." He just blurted it out. "I can't do this for much longer."

"You're what?" said Trudy. He could see the look in her eyes: *Thirty. Christ.* Then she said it. "I didn't think you were that old."

"I feel a hundred." Jules smiled a very small smile. His head was pounding. It was the truth. He felt at least one hundred years old.

"We saw unicorns. It was close to here. But they're not there anymore." Mercy unzipped her jacket to reveal a pink T-shirt with a sparkling rainbow iron-on on the front. "Trudy made me this shirt."

"Nice," said James. "You think she'll make me one?"

"No! They're for little girls!" cried Mercy, scandalized.

"But I like rainbows. Why can't I have one?"

"You're silly, James!" Mercy was laughing, doubled over. As if she could see it in her mind: great big tall James in a tiny tight pink rainbow T-shirt.

"Mercy, why don't you show Mark and me where you found those unicorns? Maybe they're back."

"Can I, Trudy?"

Trudy looked at James and Mark, smiles on their goofy faces, and at Mercy, sitting up as straight as she could, as if it would help. As if good posture might sway her. "OK, then. But come right back. We have to get home soon."

Mercy kissed Trudy on the cheek hard and loud and waved at Jules as she grabbed James's hand and pulled him toward the screen door and out onto the porch. Jules felt the hair on the back of his neck stand up as Trudy turned to face him across the table.

Alone at last.

BECAUSE SO MANY SAD STORIES
ARE ALMOST THE SAME

Alone at last and look at him. He was hobbled. Unable to get up from his chair without grunting like an old man, unable to get closer to her without hoisting himself onto his crutches and labouring to hop and swing over to her. It was unthinkable. Why was she way over there on the other side of the table?

"Come sit beside me."

"I'm fine here," she said. The sun was still behind her, shining in through the door. He couldn't tell if she was smiling. If she was laughing at him.

"You think I'm ridiculous."

"A little bit."

"But you don't know me."

"Nope." She had started to smile. He could hear it in her voice. He could see the shadow of it on her face.

"I'm a very interesting person."

"I have no doubt."

And so he told her the beginning of his story. His long, sad story. The apartment by the railroad tracks in Montreal. The room he shared with his brothers, the window looking out on the parking lot filled with garbage.

How the trains shook his bed at night the way the engines of the ships had shaken hers. How they chased rats for fun, built go-karts out of scraps they found in the alleyways. How he quit school in sixth grade and worked as a grocery-store delivery boy.

He told her about the school where nuns smacked him on the back of the head with rulers, called him stupid, dirty, and bad. Which maybe he was. Which maybe he still was. How, like Trudy, he had never known his father. He had, in fact, never heard a word about him. Didn't even know his name.

How his mother left and came back and left and came back until the boys were half crazy, half wild.

Then one day she left and she didn't come back.

He told Trudy how, after that, they never, ever answered the door. How the police came one day (he never knew why — to kick them out? To take them away? To bring some terrible news of their mother?) and they crept out onto the fire escape, scurried down the metal stairs, jumped down to the pavement, and scattered like alley cats, knowing they should never go back to the apartment again.

That they would have to make their way in the world now.

He told her how before long he had lost track of his brothers and never heard from them again.

(He didn't tell her that he was sure that he had never mattered very much to anyone. And that now he suspected he mattered nothing at all. He didn't tell her how sorry he felt for himself sometimes.)

Trudy stood up and walked around the table, sat in the chair next to his. She put her hand, palm up, on his thigh. He put his hand in hers and squeezed. His breath caught in his throat. He didn't dare speak. What was it about beautiful women that made him want to cry like a baby? What purpose could it possibly serve?

He thought he could hear voices outside, so he leaned in to kiss her before the moment passed. She pulled her head back, eluding him. And then she smiled. "I think I hear Mercy."

"Just one," he said. "Quick."

And like magic, she closed her eyes, leaned toward him, and put her soft lips on his.

Rainbows. Unicorns. Pure, hot, joy.

Then the screen door opened and let in the noise.

TRUDY

BECAUSE EVEN MONSTERS CAN BE LOVABLE

"What in the name of Jesus Christ is that?" Trudy was astounded.

"It's a *dog*, Trudy!" Mercy was dancing around the enormous wrinkled lump of brown-and-white hide that was sprawled on the living room carpet. "Her name is *Speckles*!" Mercy knelt on the floor and laid her head on the dog's back. The creature raised its big head and looked at Trudy with baggy, bloodshot eyes. "She's a *puppy*, Trudy! She's a basset hound! I LOVE HER!" The dog grunted and sighed, laid its chin back down on the ground, eyes still fixed on Trudy.

"OK, OK, pipe down a bit, Mercy." Trudy's head was pounding. She could not see how this could be a puppy. It was huge. Over two feet long and fat, it probably outweighed Mercy by twenty pounds. Puppy! It looked like a frigging monster. A gargoyle.

Its short legs splayed outward.

Its feet looked webbed.

It smelled like a wet skunk. And raw meat.

"Where's Grandma?"

"She's upstairs. I'm just taking care of the baby." Mercy patted the dog firmly on the top of the head and the dog squinted with pleasure.

Baby! thought Trudy. *God help us all.*

BECAUSE YOU SHOULD BE
CAREFUL WHAT YOU WISH FOR

Trudy, Claire, and Mercy were sitting at the kitchen table. It was weekday dinnertime, and Claire was waxing sentimental. "I always thought I would have another baby."

"Mom. Come on. What are you talking about?"

"I always thought I would have a third baby. A boy. I would have named him Jerome."

"Like the giraffe!" said Mercy.

Claire laughed. "Yeah, that's right, Mercy! Just like the giraffe!"

Trudy rolled her eyes. Mercy rolled a meatball back and forth between her fork and knife.

Claire shot a look at Trudy. "It could still happen, you know. I'm not too old."

"Baby Jerome," sang Mercy. "Somebody younger than me!"

"He would be your uncle, Mercy. A baby uncle. What do you think of that?"

"That's funny, Grandma Claire."

"That's one way of looking at it." Trudy pushed her chair back from the table. She picked up her plate and walked over to the sink. "This conversation is ridiculous."

"Why? Because I want something good to happen?" Claire

was standing now, arms rigid at her sides. Tears filled her eyes, and she let out a little sob. Startled, Speckles got up from her cushion in the corner of the kitchen and walked over to stand beside Claire. She lifted her big, heavy head and looked from Claire to Trudy still standing by the sink, plate in hand. Mercy put down her fork and knife.

"Have you completely lost your mind?" Trudy shook her head. "You can't be serious."

"It's OK, Grandma. Trudy's just tired. She doesn't mean it. You can have a baby if you want to."

"Oh my god."

"You can be very cold, Trudy. And you lack imagination. Our lives could be completely different in a couple of years, you never know. *You don't know.*" Claire's chin started to tremble again.

Mercy got up from the table and walked over to her grandmother. "Come on, Grandma Claire. Me and Speckles want to watch TV." She grabbed Claire's hand and led her out of the room. She looked back at Trudy and scowled.

Trudy turned her back on them and filled the sink.

For the love of Christ, she thought. *Where are the grown-ups?*

BECAUSE YOU LEARN SOMETHING NEW EVERY DAY

Trudy was back on Old Murphy Road again, pulling over onto the gravel shoulder. The sun was setting. She had left Mercy and Claire at home with their smelly dog and their fantasy baby, Jerome.

As she walked toward the porch, she could hear their voices, their laughter, and stopped for a second. Why was she here? She turned and looked back out over the bay and considered leaving. Just going back home. But instead she took one step at a time up to the porch, quietly, stealthily. She stood at the screen door, thinking it would be funny to just wait there until someone noticed her. Maybe give them a little fright. She saw Jules, leaning back from the table, his foot in its cast resting on a chair. He was smiling.

And then she saw something amazing, something she never thought she would see: James and Mark cuddled up together on the old couch against the back wall of the kitchen.

Those two big grown men, pressed right up against each other. Mark had his arm behind James across the back of the couch and his leg draped over James's thigh. He was almost sitting on his lap.

She turned away and crept down the steps.

Then she turned around and walked right back up the stairs, making plenty of noise and thinking, *I don't know anything about anything. Not one thing about anything in this whole world.* James opened the door before she even knocked. "It's a woman," he said. "Thank God. Come in. We were getting tired of our own company around here." She doubted this, but she liked the way it made her feel when he said it. Jules looked at her and smiled, patted his lap, and nodded at her. She walked over and settled her weight on top of him. Trudy saw him wince a little and she started to get off but he grabbed her hips and brought her back down. "No," he said. "It's good. It feels good." James grabbed Mark's hand and led him out of the room. Trudy stared after them.

"Never mind them," said Jules. "They're always like that. All over each other."

Trudy didn't know what to say.

Jules looked her in the eye. "What's up? You OK?"

"Yeah. I guess I just never really thought about it before."

"Never really thought about what?"

"You know, being gay. Around here, it's just a name people call each other, a joke. I never really thought about it being real."

Jules was laughing now. He couldn't help it.

"Don't laugh at me!" Jules pulled her close and kissed her. She kissed him back and thought about James and Mark. About them kissing. Their faces rough against each other. Their strong arms around each other. Jules's breath was hot in her ear and he was kissing her neck, his hands on her thighs. "Stay with me," he said. "Come upstairs with me."

"I can't. I have to go to work." Her body felt heavy, magnetized. Like she would have to be hauled off him with a crane. He was kissing her again, and his hands were under her shirt, undoing her bra, his fingers tracing a line down her sides, barely touching the sides of her breasts. His voice was in her ear again. "I will make you feel good, I promise."

Trudy kissed his neck, his cheek, his ear, and pulled away. "I've heard that one before," she said.

(This was a lie.

Nobody had ever said anything like that to her before. Ever.)

She shrugged her shoulders as she did up her bra, straightened her shirt, and flipped her hair back over her shoulders. She grabbed her fringed purse and headed for the door.

"Promises, promises."

BECAUSE IT DOESN'T TAKE MUCH

Driving back home, Trudy thought, *it didn't take much.*

That face, that body. That voice. The freckles on his arms.

A sad story, a sly look.

A deep kiss. A light, glancing touch.

The promise of pleasure and the spectre of a terrible, violent, public death to make it all ridiculous, sad, pointless. Irresistible.

Just these things and the sailing arc of cupid's arrow and she was done for.

Lost.

Stupid, stricken, sick with love.

BECAUSE THAT'S LIFE

Trudy sat on the edge of the tub, put the stopper in, and turned on the water. She let it run over her hand, cold at first, slowly warming up. When the water was a few inches deep, she swirled it around the tub with her hand, mixing the cool with the hot. "Mercy! Bath's ready!"

Mercy came padding into the small bathroom, pink bathrobe crisscrossed over her little body, belt pulled tight around her waist, matching pink slippers slapping against her feet. Trudy grabbed the end of her belt and pulled her close, squeezing her. There was something about the way Mercy did these things so precisely — tying her robe, combing her hair, the careful, systematic way she divided the food on her plate into sections before eating it, one tidy bite at a time — that made Trudy want to cry. It was so strange, so at odds with everything and everybody around her.

"Trudy, you're crushing me!"

Trudy let her go.

"Trudy, can I have bubbles? Please? *Please!* Please, Trudy." Mercy was standing on her tiptoes, bouncing, trying to reach the box of bubble bath on the shelf behind the toilet.

"Alright, alright." Trudy got the box down and sprinkled the blue powder under the running water.

"More! More! Trudy, I want the bubbles to reach here!" Mercy was waving her hand high above her head. Dancing from foot to foot.

"OK, lady. That's enough. Get in there."

Mercy took off her robe and hung it on the doorknob, kicked off her slippers and stepped into the tub. She carefully skimmed the surface of the water, pushing all the foamy white bubbles toward the front of the tub, piling them up high in a mound, then gathering up handfuls to put on each shoulder, on the top of her head, on each knee. Singing quietly to herself, "Who loves bubbles? I love bubbles . . ." She patted a handful of foam carefully onto her face, making a beard and moustache.

Trudy lowered the lid on the toilet and sat down, lighting a cigarette and throwing the match into the sink. Watching Mercy in the bath, slippery and perfect as a seal, she wondered — against her will and in the strange detached way she always thought about this — about the baby she could have had. Would it have been another girl or, unimaginably, a boy? Could she and Claire have cared for both kids, Mercy and the other one?

Maybe, if Trudy had kept the baby, Tammy would have stayed to help out instead of taking off. Maybe Claire would be able to make it through the day without crying her eyes out.

And maybe Santa Claus would come on a magic sleigh pulled by a red-nosed reindeer to give them a million dollars and they would all live happily ever after in Fairy Land.

Tra-la-la.

"OK, champ. I think you're clean enough now." Trudy ran her cigarette butt under the tap in the sink and threw it in the trash can, rinsed the ashes down the drain.

"No, Trudy! Not yet!"

"I have to go to work, Mercy." Trudy reached in the tub and turned over Mercy's small hands. "Look at your hands, they're like prunes!"

"They're not!" They weren't. But that was life. Trudy had to go to work.

She pulled the plug while Mercy wailed, "*Nooooo!*"

Trudy held out a towel, and Mercy dejectedly stepped into her aunt's arms and put her head on her shoulder. "I love you, Trudy, but you're mean."

"I know, pal. I love you, too. Bed time."

BECAUSE REAL LOVE IS
ALWAYS MIXED WITH TERROR

Mercy loved to ask questions. She was a question machine. Spitting out question after question after follow-up question. What's that? Who's that? What are you doing? What's Grandma doing? Why? It had started early, as soon as she could talk. And that's when Tammy had disappeared — when the questions started.

Trudy remembered every detail, every moment, of the day Mercy was born. Her memory of that day had a special glassy clarity about it. A bright, crisp September morning. There had been a chill in the air. The smell of wet leaves and cut grass. A bright blue sky and the sun sparkling on the river as they drove to the hospital. Trudy was driving, Claire was fidgeting in the passenger seat, and Tammy was a writhing mass filling the back seat, her soft face turned to the ceiling, appealing to her saviour.

"Jesus Christ! Jesus. God*damn!*"

"Almost there, Tammy. Hold on," said Claire. Trudy turned on the radio. The Bee Gees, Captain & Tennille. It made her cringe. Her kingdom for some rock and roll. Claire was on her knees, turned around, facing the back seat.

"Fuck ME, that hurts!"

"Tammy, that's horrible. Please. Think of the baby."

"*Urgh!* Mom! How can I think about anything else?"

Trudy turned the radio off and rolled her window down and breathed in the fragrant autumn air. The baby, the baby. How could any of them possibly think of anything else?

And then the hospital.

That same hospital in Harristown. Dirty white paint flaking off the red-brick exterior. Stone steps worn smooth in the middle by generations of shuffling patients, the hollow makeshift wooden ramp on the side. Lit-up exit signs boxed in with wire grates. Pale yellow walls and grey and white and black speckled terrazzo floors. In reception, there were nurses with white caps, spotless white belted dresses, white stockings, and flat white rubber-bottomed shoes. The ones smocked in dull green did their work elsewhere, out of sight.

Trudy remembered.

As her sister was admitted — as Tammy testily answered the nurse's questions between the painful waves of her contractions — Trudy could think only one thought: she is here for *this* and I was here for *that*. *What a distance there was*, she thought, *between this and that.*

And when it was all over,

when Tammy was sleeping, her cheeks still purple-red from pushing,

when Trudy took the baby from her sleeping sister's arms,

when she ran her hand over the tiny baby's head and smoothed down her sparse, soft, dark hair,

when Trudy held that baby against her breast, leaned in and smelled her skin, kissed her plump cheek, she had felt something new. This was a new kind of love. The kind that was mixed with terror.

Mercy, she thought. *God, have mercy on this child. Make her different from us. Make her better, stronger, faster.*

Make her relentless and clever and mighty.

And she would be. She was.

Trudy knew it right away. Mercy was all that and much, much more.

BECAUSE EVERYBODY REMEMBERS EVERYTHING

On her weekend off, Trudy drove Mercy to the Point to see the boats. The sun was getting warmer now, making her believe that summer was possible after all. They rolled down their windows and reclined in their seats and waited for a ship to come through the locks. The light on the rippling water was blinding. Mercy shielded her eyes with one hand, looking east then west, licking her pistachio ice cream with her already-green tongue. She ordered it every time; mostly, because of the colour.

"I remember my mom, Trudy."

"I know. Me, too."

"She had brown hair like mine. Light brown."

"Yup."

"She was pretty."

"That's true."

"She gave me a necklace." Mercy touched her throat. "Where *is* my necklace, Trudy?"

"Not sure, babe. It's around somewhere. We can look when we get home." Trudy remembered the necklace, too. A tiny silver shamrock pendant with a fake emerald, on a short silver chain. In some box or drawer or jam jar somewhere in that house. Needle in a shit-stack.

"It's not lost," asserted Mercy.

"No."

"Maybe my mom is lost."

"No, I'm pretty sure she knows her way home. It just might take her a little while, that's all. She'll be back." Spoken with less conviction than she would have liked, than Mercy would have liked, but Trudy had never been a great pretender. She made an attempt at distraction. "Should we go see those unicorns again tomorrow?"

"Sure," said Mercy, staring out the windshield. "I can show everybody my necklace!"

Trudy looked out her window at the water, glittering gold, the sun lifting a bit of mist off the surface. As always, the boat came from the direction you weren't looking in. It came toward the back of her turned head, its enormous bow looming up out of the distance, wedging into the narrow channel.

Its smokestack-topped stern as big as a high-rise apartment building, unmoored from a city street and floating away down the river.

Away, away. Always away.

BECAUSE IF YOU LOOK HARD
ENOUGH IT IS PROBABLY THERE

And there it was. After an hour of searching, there it was in the back corner of the bedroom closet. There, tangled in the deep shag of the carpet, its chain a complicated snare of a knot. Trudy, her bare knees being tattooed by the carpet, leaned down onto her elbows and pulled the shamrock necklace carefully away. She sat cross-legged on the floor and started at the knot. Mercy crawled over, knelt down right beside her, and put her head against her shoulder, watching every move. "You can fix it. Right, Trudy?"

"Not if I can't use my arms. Shove over." Mercy moved over a bit, folded over on herself, and rested her forehead on her knees. She stayed very still. Praying, possibly.

Finally, Trudy put her hand under Mercy's chin and lifted it up. "There. See?" The necklace dangled off the end of her index finger, the green stone glinting in the light. Mercy held her hair up off the back of her neck and let her aunt put the necklace on.

"Never taking it off now, Trudy!"

"That's right, pal."

"Even when I take a bath."

"Sure."

"Thank you, Trudy." Mercy said this with alarming seriousness, her small hand on her heart.

"No sweat." Trudy pulled Mercy close for a bone-crushing squeeze. She hated her sister sometimes. Most of the time, really.

TAMMY
(AND FENTON)

BECAUSE THERE IS ANOTHER
SKIN BENEATH YOUR SKIN

If you followed the bank of the river to the west, only thirty miles away from Preston Mills, you would find Tammy, in Brockville, Ontario. She worked in a strip club but was not a stripper. She was something even dumber than that: she was a topless waitress. Serving drinks, emptying ashtrays, wiping up tables, taking crap from drunken idiots. All with her shirt off. In a bar called Jiggles.

Dumbest job ever.

When she had first started working at the bar, she had felt so exposed, like she had been peeled. She didn't know how to stand, how to walk, how to bend over and pick things up. Everything felt like a pose. And she couldn't keep her eyes off the girls on the stage, their legs in the air, opening and closing like fans. But it didn't take long to forget, for it all to seem normal. For the dancers to fade into the background. For her own skin to start to feel like a uniform she slipped into at the start of each shift.

Until the day she met Fenton. Fucking Fenton.

A mouse of a man, sitting with a loud tangle of municipal workers in the back corner of the bar. One night, he had detached himself from the group and started following her around. Clearing tables for her, helping her restock the bar at the end of the night, asking her questions about her life. Her family. And suddenly, she felt nude all over again. And angry. And in love.

In love with Fenton Osborne. How could it be? Short and skinny, crazy as a loon. But he just wore away at her like sandpaper on a board until everything was smooth and easy and she couldn't imagine her life without him anymore.

BECAUSE YOU DON'T KNOW WHAT MAKES IT HAPPEN

Fenton had problems. Nobody could argue otherwise. He lacked ambition and he smoked a lot of pot. When Fenton was alone and when he smoked pot, he was not nervous. Take away either of these variables, and he was quite nervous indeed. It had always been this way. When he was a kid, he couldn't talk without pacing. He would look to the ground, thinking about what he should say, and the second he started speaking, at the sound of his own voice, he would begin to walk in circles. His mother used to grab his hands before asking him a question so that he would stay still when he answered her. It made him feel like he was going to explode.

But in spite of his nature and his habits, as a grown man, Fenton had found a way to be happy. He was in love and he had a job. Each day, he got up, put on his coveralls, and walked out into the sunshine. Or into the rain or sleet or snow, depending on the season. He smoked a joint as he walked to the depot and got into a truck. He cut grass, raked leaves, flooded rinks, plowed the streets. Some days, he washed windows or picked up litter from the side of the road with a spike at the end of a wooden pole. He was almost always outside, and he was almost always alone. All of this was good.

Until the spells started again.

Last week, for example, he was cutting grass. It was bright mid-morning, and he was driving the tractor across the wide green expanse of St. Lawrence Park. He headed slowly toward the river, turned to the right, and rode along the bank, getting as close as possible to the rocky shore, then turned to the right again toward the town. He was riding up and down over gentle hills, turning right and right again in diminishing rectangles around the park, making semi-circular detours around trees, leaving dark green lines of cuttings on the bright green grass. The air smelled of grass, brine, sunlight, and soil. He was alone and his heart was happy.

Fenton turned off the mower and stepped down from the tractor. A giant laker was edging into view from the west. A long red-and-white ship against the grey-blue water and the clear blue sky. Black smokestack high at the stern. Fenton leaned on his rake and watched the big boat go by, feeling the thrum of the engine pulsing through the earth under his feet. It had taken ten, maybe fifteen minutes for the ship to pass out of sight. He watched the blunt, cut-off stern of the boat as it moved away, the sun in his eyes. Like a factory on the water, his mother used to say. That working on boats was just like working in a factory, only on the water. Fenton didn't think this could be true. Not entirely. Not when you could walk out onto the deck and smell the water, see the cities and towns go by. Houses and farms and forests all crowded up to the very edge of the land. Dogs in yards, cows in fields like specks. You couldn't see or smell anything in a factory except the factory. He knew that from experience.

Dragging his rake across the grass, Fenton felt it beginning. Maybe it was the vibration of the ship that brought it on. He didn't know why the spells came, but he knew that if one came, others were likely to follow. One after another, day after day until they went away for a month or two.

Here it was. He could see it and he could hear it. There was a high sound like the breezy summer air had crystallized and was ringing like a million tiny bells. The edges of things glittered and sparked and magnified. He could see everything in a sharp, sparkling light. The cut end of each blade of grass, the grain of the wood of the rake handle, the web of tiny diamond-shaped lines on the backs of his hands. This was it.

Fenton's knees buckled and he fell onto the grass. He was out.

When he woke up, there would be a sharp pain in his head. He would have trouble with numbers for a few days. Nothing would sound right. And he would long to get it back, that dreamy, spacy feeling that knocked him out cold.

It was as though the universe had allowed him to step out of the stream of time for a moment, to be suspended and let it all flow past him. Every time it happened, it came as a great relief.

BECAUSE YOU'RE NOBODY'S BABY

Tammy understood very well the desire to step out of your life, to resist the current dragging you forward. Or down.

It was safe to say that motherhood was not what she had expected. Not that she had spent a great deal of time thinking about it, even when she was pregnant. Being pregnant felt like a dream. It had all seemed so unbelievable, so absurd: her pumpkin belly, her enormous breasts, the baby moving around in there. She could actually see it moving, pressing against her flesh from the inside, creating humps and ripples across her stomach. Even watching this — the movements of the baby inside her body — even when the contractions started, the whole idea had seemed far-fetched. Like science fiction. A practical joke.

She had spent the first six months of her pregnancy brainwashing herself into believing it was not really happening at all. Her periods had stopped, and everything started tasting like aluminum foil. She started eating only peanut butter on toast and bananas. She drank only cold milk or ginger ale. When her bras stopped fitting, she went to Beamish and bought stretchy ones. Likewise, her jeans. She mentioned none of this to anyone. She did not even allow the words to form inside her own head.

Until one morning, her mother stopped her in the kitchen, her hands heavy on both of Tammy's shoulders, and she started to cry. Tammy told her to stop blubbering and get off. But the jig was up.

Predictably, the news spread through Preston Mills like proverbial wildfire. It was spread with joy and sanctimony. As though the words were printed on ticker tape — Tammy Johnson is pregnant! — and floats paraded through the town, showering the news over everybody. *It serves her right*, Tammy supposed was the general feeling. Though Preston Mills seemed to relish the idea of an impregnated Tammy, they did not favour being faced with her real fleshy self. At first, she almost enjoyed the discomfort she caused people on the street, but the novelty soon wore off.

Three boys who had slept with her had pre-emptively denied being the father of the baby. Several boys who had not slept with her had also stepped into the spotlight and made passionate denials. Her boyfriend of the moment, Gary Petty, evaporated in a puff of Player's Light Navy Cut smoke. Tammy quit her job at the gas station and camped out on the couch. Her mother made casseroles. Trudy, the centre of the universe, acted like the whole situation was a personal insult, a plot designed to make her life more difficult.

And when the baby was born in a flash of terrible blinding pain — brilliant in the seemingly endless tedium of the crushing pain of labour — when they finally handed the baby to Tammy, she felt cold panic spread through her chest. What went through her mind was this: *It isn't mine. This isn't my baby.* She stared at the baby and the baby stared back, and she thought:

This is not mine.

Later, when the baby cried, warm milk would soak the front of Tammy's shirt, turning cold and sticky within seconds. Cursing, she would storm upstairs to change her shirt while Trudy or Claire warmed a bottle, scooped up the baby, and fed her.

Even though Tammy would stay for almost three more years, she was already never there. They were already getting along just fine without her.

BECAUSE IT CAN NEVER BE FAR ENOUGH

It was the middle of winter when Tammy left. She got ready to go to work at the gas station as usual. She picked up Mercy and gave her a quick squeeze before trying to set her down. The toddler cried and tugged on her shirt, grabbing at her pant legs as she headed for the door. All business, Claire picked Mercy up and headed toward the kitchen. Trudy was upstairs in bed. Nobody said goodbye as Tammy stepped out into the freezing January morning, the cold air making her shaky breath visible.

Claire and Trudy had been angry with her for months, pouring on the guilt. Tammy had been out a lot lately, had started not coming home after work once a week, twice a week. And she found that the more time she spent away from home, the better she felt.

So, that morning, while Trudy slept, Tammy shuffled around the darkened bedroom, packing a bag. Some of her own things, some of Trudy's. She brought the bag downstairs and put it by the door in plain sight. Who would notice with the amount of junk jammed into the tiny entryway? When she left for work, Claire was so caught up in comforting poor Mercy, in showing Tammy how it was done, she didn't notice the bag. Had she even noticed her leaving? Tammy doubted it. She left the house. She worked her shift, and at quitting time, she just waited around in the parking lot in front of the garage. When the Voyageur bus pulled up, she got on it.

She hoisted her bag onto the rack and settled into her seat. She watched thirty miles of grey-blue river go by her window, then the low stone walls of the outskirts of Brockville, with its psychiatric hospital, its boarding school for girls. A movie theatre, a dairy bar, a strip club, a row of shops. The courthouse. The bus pulled to a stop outside another gas station, and she hauled herself up and walked down the aisle, down the steps, and out onto the gravel lot. Snow was starting to fall in big fat fluffy flakes, glowing in the beams of the street lights.

It wasn't very far from home. Not nearly far enough. But it was a start.

BECAUSE YOU FEEL THE ONLY FEELING YOU CAN BEAR

Her baby would be five years old soon. One year, eight months. That was how long it had been since Tammy had seen her child. Or her own mother or her sister. She tried not to think about Mercy, but every time she did, she felt angry. There was a series of micro-emotions — passing almost too quickly to be detected — between the idea or image of her daughter coming to mind and the feeling of burning, sickening anger. These feelings probably included love, guilt, anxiety, and simple sad longing, but none of them stuck. Anger was the one that took hold.

Anger was the only one she could bear.

BECAUSE SOMETIMES IT ALL MIXES TOGETHER

The sound of the smoke alarm was almost drowning out the sound of the timer on the stove. Fenton could hear both now, one on top of the other.

"Fucking retard."

"I didn't hear it!"

"How is that possible?" Tammy pulled open the oven door and thick black smoke rolled out like thunderclouds. She launched the tray of desiccated fish sticks and sent it sailing through the air. Fenton ducked as the smoking tray spun over his head and bounced off the wall behind him. He stared at the tray on the carpet and at the scattered charcoal-crusted rectangles of fish. The light was catching in the threads of the carpet, in the crispy black coating of the fish. Gold light was pouring in from all sides, filling in all the spaces between all the objects he could see.

"I don't believe this."

The alarm stuttered and Tammy's voice became slower, deeper. Fenton leaned back against the couch and looked at her through the golden haze. She was just standing there, hands on her hips.

"The parade is on Sunday," he said, eyelashes fluttering.

"Fantastic," said Tammy.

"The fish will be there."

"Great. Perfect."

"And pumpkin pie."

Fenton thought he could hear a great cheer rising up from a crowd as he closed his eyes, as the room shuddered to the right and toppled him sideways onto the floor.

BECAUSE SOMETIMES YOU DON'T KNOW
WHAT'S HAPPENING UNTIL IT'S OVER

He knew it was a bad idea. It couldn't be worse, really. But Fenton couldn't help himself. This was the fourth time this week. He parked the truck at the yard and walked the wrong way. Instead of walking home to where Tammy was waiting — likely fuming, she was always fuming lately — he walked three blocks in the wrong direction, then turned north. The idea was to travel north in as straight a line as possible, no matter what got in his way. He walked between two red-brick houses, then climbed a fence, walked through a flower bed, across the lawn, splashed through an old plastic wading pool, through another flower bed, over another fence. Down the alley. He walked across the street, between the houses, through another yard, and scrambled up onto the roof of a shed and jumped to another shed in another yard. And so on. Until he was north of town on the other side of the highway, climbing over barbed-wire fences and walking through the yellow-green pastures.

North, north.

Field after field. Birds chirping. Crickets making noise. The grassy field soft and springy beneath his wet work boots. Then through the pines into the clearing before the crunch of the gravel beside the railway tracks. Fenton bent down and placed a hand on the metal rail. It was warm from the sun even though the air was a bit cool. It was smooth and quiet and still. He stepped into the middle of the tracks and sat down, cross-legged. Then he laid down flat on his back.

With one hand on each rail, he looked up at the blue sky. Bright white feathery wisps of clouds. The crickets sang and the grass made a whispery dry brushing sound. The high tops of the pines seemed to sway dark against the blue sky. He could feel it coming. The softest subtlest vibration in his fingertips. So soft, so subtle, it might not be real. Just a watery ripple in the clear late afternoon air.

He loved it. The feeling that filled him. Bliss. The weakness in his knees, the trembling of the ground, the black wings folding inward, blocking the light. He was sinking. He was fading away.

Fenton forced his eyes open but could see nothing. White light. The trembling hum loud in his ears. He forced himself up on his elbows, tucked the toe of his boot under the outside of the rail, and rolled himself over onto the gravel. He could feel the stones through his shirt, sharp against his chest. He pushed his boot against the rail and he rolled down the gravel bank, tumbling down the slope until he was lying under the pines. A bed of needles beneath him.

And he was gone, gone.

Out for the count.

By the time Fenton opened his eyes, rolled over onto his knees, and stood up, brown pine needles dropping off the back of his shirt, the train was long gone. The spectacular rush of earth-quaking car after car blurring by, the screech of metal on metal, was over. There was only a faint rumbling echo in the distance, a lonely throb in the air far, far away. He was a stiff scarecrow standing in a field. A shadow in the twilight.

His headache followed him all the way home.

BECAUSE THE IMPOSSIBLE IS NOT THE POSSIBLE

Tammy's throat was sore, her voice hoarse from shouting. Tears were drying on her cheeks as she swept the kitchen floor, the strokes of the broom getting less effective, more violent, until she lost control completely and threw the broom at the wall. She looked around for something else to throw, something to break, but stopped herself. She stood, hands on hips, breathing hard and shaking her head at the universe, at life. Terrified, Fenton slipped out the back door, pulling his jacket on as he took the back steps two at a time, jogging down the alley. He would come back later when the air had cleared. Bearing milk and tea bags. Some cookies if he had enough cash. Peace offerings to the furious power inhabiting his home.

She watched him through the kitchen window, trotting across the parking lot. Scooting away with his tail between his legs. Fenton Osborne. The latest in a relatively long line of utterly confounding men inhabiting Tammy's bed. Not for the first time she wondered what exactly it was she wanted from him. What she had ever wanted from men. It seemed to her that men were always so certain about what they wanted. In her experience, anyway, it was usually something simple. And stupid.

They wanted you to take your clothes off slowly and walk toward them. Or walk away from them. To leave your shoes on, leave your bra on, your pantyhose, whatever. They wanted you to look at them or not to look at them.

To talk or not to say a word.

To touch them or stop touching them.

To kneel or bend over.

Whatever it was, it was usually enunciated clearly and easily done.

But what did she want? Mostly, she wanted to be loved and left alone. Not sequentially, but simultaneously. In equal measure. Love me. *And leave me the fuck alone.* It made her feel itchy, swarmed, irritated most of the time.

Fenton, ever accommodating, just wanted what she wanted. Whatever it could possibly be. Mostly, he wanted peace, which was not available. What had he done this time to get himself in so much trouble? He had made a simple suggestion. He had just pointed out that since they both had steady jobs and now that they were settled in this ground-floor apartment that backed onto an alley, Mercy could come and stay with them sometimes. Maybe just on weekends.

Five, four, three, two, one.

Tammy had detonated. Wept. Cursed. Fenton had scooted out the door. The broom had hit the wall. The shit, the fan. Et cetera. Poor Fenton. He had guessed wrong again.

It would not stop him from trying, though. He was nothing if not persistent.

Poor old, sad old Fenton, winding through alleyways, buying milk and tea at the corner store, trying to cook up another scheme to make his woman happy, to make the impossible possible.

MERCY

BECAUSE NOTHING IS EVER QUITE
THE WAY YOU WANT IT TO BE

For the record, this is what Mercy thought. She thought that nothing was ever quite the way you wanted it to be. It could be close. But it was never right. She had Trudy and Grandma, but she wanted her mother. Or for her mother to be dead and Trudy to be her mother. She felt bad for thinking this, but she thought it sometimes anyway.

She wanted people to listen to her. They did. But they always laughed. They never just listened and understood and answered back to her in a way that helped. She could never say things in a way that didn't make grown-ups laugh.

Mercy wanted to stay up late, to eat more candy, to do things by herself. She wanted her own room, but she was scared to be alone in the dark. She wanted there to be no such thing as dying, even if there was such a thing as God in Heaven.

She wanted school to start in August, not September, so she could go sooner. She wanted to have long shining hair. Trudy's hair was thick and dark and shiny and her ponytail was as thick as Mercy's wrist. Like the tail of a real pony. Mercy's hair was light brown, a little bit greyish like a mouse, and so thin that her ears poked through at the sides. When Trudy put Mercy's hair back in a ponytail, it was a scraggly little mouse tail.

For her birthday last year, she had asked for a purse, picturing herself walking around with Trudy's big, slouchy brown leather bag over her shoulder, tossing her hair back, digging around in there for some gum or a nickel. (But not cigarettes. She was never going to smoke. The smell was awful.) But when she had opened her present from Grandma Claire, it was a tiny plastic pink-and-white purse. A toy purse. With a cartoon lamb on the front. It made her feel like a baby. But she still said thank you. She still climbed into her grandma's lap and kissed her on the cheek. She still carried the purse around everywhere she went, put Chiclets and pennies and a tiny doll-mirror in there. A key she found along the side of the road. She pretended it was a little bit different, turned the lamb side toward her body so nobody could see it. She made do.

In September, she would be five. She tried not to get her hopes up about presents.

Mercy wanted everything to be right. She wanted everyone to be happy. She wanted the adults to pair off like dance partners, like in a fairy tale. Trudy should marry Jules. Trudy's father should come home and marry Grandma Claire. Her mom should come home married to a rich prince who would buy them a big house with canopy beds and a swimming pool.

They would have more puppies. And kittens. Both.

She should be allowed to go to school right now. Today.

And Jules should not be allowed to try to jump over the river in a car. She couldn't understand why he wanted to do it. And she couldn't understand why other people wanted him to do it. There was something mean about that. Cruel. *Heartless* is what Trudy said.

But none of these things were up to Mercy. Nothing in the whole world was up to her. She was not in charge. She wanted to be in charge.

Mercy wanted those white horses to have horns. Why shouldn't they?

JULES

BECAUSE DREAMS CAN MARCH
RIGHT INTO THE DAYLIGHT

Jules was not in charge either. That much was clear. Things were
not going according to plan.

He needed three things to get this stunt done: a car, a ramp,
himself. None was in good shape. All through the month of June, it
had rained. It rained so much that a sort of lake had formed in the
low-lying field alongside the ramp. By the end of the month, the
mud was so deep that trucks had to be brought in to pull the tractors
out, then bigger tractors had to be brought in to pull the trucks out.
Construction came to a halt. Costs were out of control. Investors
were pulling out. The TV people were getting nervous.

On Dominion Day, about a thousand pounds of packed earth
slid off the side of the ramp, revealing unmoored steel girders.
The asphalt on top tore in two. The engineer was fired. The construction company declined to extend its contract. The jump was
postponed. July 15th became August 19th.

It was all slipping away from him now. Jules knew it. Before
the TV deal, before the promoter got involved, Jules had been in
charge. There hadn't been much to be in charge of — a few small
investors, a fake car, his own carnival sideshow patter — but the
project had been his. Now arrangements were made by someone

else. Decisions were taken without him. The promoter recruited investors, hired contractors, worked with the network to schedule interviews and appearances, set the date for the jump. And then cancelled it. And then set a new one.

The only person Jules knew how to contact was Sammy Harrison, and he could never get a straight answer about Sammy. Did he work for the network? The promoter? Who was paying him? He had just started popping up one day, all feathered hair and smiles and tight T-shirts. He was everywhere. At the jump site, at press events. And now he was calling from Chicago, where the rocket car was being built. He had been talking to the head mechanic and test driver. Twice they had tested the car. Twice the gas tank had exploded. But they had it all figured out now. No need to worry. Sammy had everything under control. Next week, he said, Jules should be able to test drive it himself. Jules had never driven a rocket car before. Apparently, this one could go 270 miles an hour.

The ramp was being rebuilt using as much of the existing materials as possible. There was a new engineer, a new construction company. A few days of sunshine, and the site was starting to dry up a little. He allowed himself to feel hope.

Then one night, just a week before the new date, Jules went to the site and drove his car halfway up the ramp. The pavement was covered in cracks and patches. It was a mess. The ride was so bumpy it rattled his teeth. He put the car in park and sat there, leaning back into his seat, staring at the moon hanging in the sky like a yellow light bulb. A dark shadowy ring of black clouds surrounded it. Slowly shuttered around it, blotting out the light.

He wasn't surprised when Sammy called to deliver the news. The jump would have to be delayed again. Maybe to the end of September.

Trudy was happy each time the jump was delayed — which was flattering — but she was in the minority in Preston Mills. Jules saw the way people looked at him. Like him, he supposed, they were starting to think the jump might never happen. That the whole thing was a hoax.

When his cast came off, his ankle looked shrunken. The skin was shrivelled and white, and he seemed to have grown an extra layer of dark hair where the cast had been. It was disgusting.

Limping through the grocery store one day, a boy called out to him. He was maybe twelve years old.

"Hey! Jules Tremblay!"

"Yeah?"

"You're a fuckin' *chicken*!" The kid ran off to join his friends on the sidewalk outside of the store, flapping his arms like wings. Laughing his head off.

And Jules limped along behind his shopping cart like a sad old woman.

(And he felt like he had had this dream before. This dream of being broken, deflated, unmanned in a grocery store. In a town full of strangers. This dream and the one about the crumpling of the hood and the crushing of bones, the smack of his helmet against the wheel and then the smell of gas. The rasp and click of the lighter. This and all the other bad endings or bad beginnings: the ramp sinking into the mud, leaning to the left, the rocket car exploding on a track in Chicago in a fluttering cloud of dollar bills.

When he was a kid, he had dreams about his mother leaving him alone with his brothers. And his brothers leaving him alone in the street. Disappearing down alleyways like ghosts.

Now, he dreamed of the water. He had dreams about the cold water of the St. Lawrence River bubbling green outside the windows of the car as it sank down, down, down. And the tentacles of a monster sliding black against the windshield, shutting out the light.

And Jules thought, *most of these things have already happened.*

One by one they have marched out of the dream world and into the daylight.)

BECAUSE THERE IS ALWAYS SOMEONE
EAGER TO DELIVER BAD NEWS

The following evening, a crew filmed Jules speaking at the Preston Mills Men's Club. The club had invited him to talk about the jump at their monthly meeting. Jules brought a piece of bristol board covered with press clippings and photos of his past stunts, crowds cheering, cars flying through the air. And a poster-sized photo of the rocket car replica. (Jules wished he hadn't enlarged the photo quite so much. You could see the gaps at the seams of the turbine where it was starting to come apart. If you looked close enough, you could see that the racing stripe was made of electrical tape.)

Jules soldiered on. He talked about watching Lightning Jones on TV, jumping the fountain in Las Vegas on his motorcycle, and his boyhood dream of pulling off the greatest stunt of all time. How happy he had been to find such a perfect site for the jump in Preston Mills.

When he finished his talk, a few of the men clapped. It sounded like the beginning of rain on a tin roof. Fat, occasional drops here and there. Slap. Pause. Slap, slap, slap. There was a shifting of chairs and a rumble of voices at the back of the room.

Jules stood at the podium and waited for questions. The fluorescent lights flickered and hummed above.

"Anybody?"

At the back of the room, a big, burly wall of a man called Bill Puck leaned back in his chair and drummed his thick sausage fingers on the tabletop. Still seated, he yelled, "Hey, Tremblay!"

Jules scanned the room until he identified the speaker, saw him there, sprawled in his chair. "Yes, sir?"

"You and I have something in common."

"Really?" said Jules. "What's that?"

Giant Bill smiled a giant smile. "Neither one of us is ever gonna jump the goddamn St. Lawrence River in a fucking *car*."

BECAUSE YOU JUST KEEP MAKING THINGS UP UNTIL THEY SEEM TRUE

The cameras, the cameras. They were making his life hell. The date was set again for September 23rd and everyone seemed confident that the ramp and the car would be ready. The machine was in motion. Jules was in Ottawa, filming a *Wide World of Sports* profile, "training" for the jump. Why Ottawa? Who knew. A prettier backdrop, maybe, and better hotels for the crew. Jules stubbed out his cigarette and jogged for the camera as it rolled backward on a trolley of some kind, and he lied about the need to stay in top physical condition in order to smash himself to bits in a car. (He was winded and his gait was lopsided. But never mind.)

Then the producers had him in a kayak in the canal that wound through the city. Geese and ducks swam up to him, curious. He had insisted on a life jacket. There was something about the murkiness of the canal, the occasional flash of carp scales near the surface that unnerved him. The life jacket pushed up uncomfortably against his chin. The crew teased him, asked him if he was going to wear a life jacket on the day of the big jump. He grinned sweatily into the camera. Clearly they didn't understand the plan. "I'm not gonna kayak across the river, fellas. I'm gonna fly."

Back in Preston Mills, they took him and Trudy in a boat to the island across from the ramp, his purported landing spot. (Although Jules talked about jumping over the river and the stunt was being marketed as "The Mile Jump," the plan was to jump to an island in the middle of the river. It was not really a mile away from the shore. Probably half a mile. It was still preposterous.) He and a reporter sat on stumps on the island, tall grass waving around them, the water lapping against the shore. Trudy stood behind the cameramen. This was the first time she had seen him in promotion mode, performing for the cameras. He hoped he didn't look like he felt: a bit off, a bit sick to his stomach.

"Now, Jules, I can't help but notice that there are a fair number of trees on this island. Are you worried about that?"

"No. You see, we didn't want to disturb the landscape here too much. The car I have can be steered in the air. State of the art. The steering wheel moves the wings, so I can actually be pretty precise. Plus there's a parachute."

There was a long pause. The two men stared across the water at the ramp in the distance.

"I was actually thinking of planting roses here." Jules got up from his stump and gestured around himself, making a slow circle. He was making this up. But he liked it. He could see it in his mind. "You know, it would make the landing site easy to see from the air. And make a nice soft landing. A big long bed of red roses."

Out of the corner of his eye, Jules saw Trudy turn away from them and look toward the wide grey river. He thought he could see her shoulders begin to shake.

BECAUSE A LITTLE PROGRESS
WOULD BE NICE FOR A CHANGE

This was exactly what Jules needed: progress. Just a little progress for a change. Maybe it wasn't too much to ask after all. He
was standing on a long windblown asphalt track near a clutch of
factories in Chicago. Or close to Chicago, anyway. Sammy stood
there beside him, bouncing on the balls of his feet, hands in pockets. The car came inching out of the garage in the distance trailed
by three guys in coveralls. The car, a Lincoln Continental, was
butter yellow and gleaming. The two wings attached to the doors
were painted to match and glinted with brilliant chrome trim.
Jules sighed. It was a thing of beauty. The rumble of the engine
was deep and steady and loud as hell.

"You have a suit with you?" one of the mechanics asked Jules.
After a pause: "Like, a fire-retardant suit?" Jules did not have a
fire-retardant suit with him. On this trip. Or at all.

He was on a budget. Or, at least, he used to be. Now he was
just trying to stem the flow, trying to keep the hole from getting
so deep it swallowed him up. Jules had never been good with
money. Before he made his TV deal, he had spent every penny he
earned — and substantially more — on the fake car and his "pro-
motional tour." And when he made his TV deal, he made a bad

deal. His compensation would be based on a (small) portion of profit. As costs increased, his potential reward was reduced. And the costs were incredible. Beyond anything he had ever imagined. But at least he would get a large lump sum when — if — he completed the jump. They were no dummies at that network.

Jules shook his head, the wind blowing his hair around. "That's OK. You can use mine. Might be a bit snug, but it'll do." The man jogged away from Jules, back toward the garage.

Jules estimated that the mechanic was about six inches shorter than he was and about twenty-five pounds lighter. Oh well.

There was a cameraman there, of course, to capture Jules struggling to zip up the suit. The zipper was stuck, unflatteringly, right at the bottom of his belly and would go no further. The shoulders were very tight, and every time he shrugged or bent at the waist, the back seam was pulled a little farther up between his buttocks. He hoped there would be no shots of him from behind.

Or from the side.

Or from the front for that matter.

He gave up on the zipper and put on his helmet. The only thing that would make him feel better about anything was driving that car as fast as it would go.

Jules sat in the driver's seat and strapped in, struggling to pay attention to the instructions of the mechanic. Frankly, it was not that complicated.

It was just a car.

You still had to steer with the wheel and you still had to step on the gas. There was a button for the rocket booster and a button for the parachute. What was important, apparently, was timing. And not to use the parachute to slow down, unless he absolutely had to — it was kind of a single-use thing and it was expensive. Just get it up to speed and then start to slow down right away. It was just a test, so he could get the feel of it. They talked through it again. The mechanic ducked out of the driver's side window and stood back from the track.

Alone inside the car, Jules was sweating, talking to himself. Finally, he said: "One, two, three, *go!*" and pushed the pedal to the floor. *Fast!* The car was so fast. He pushed the booster, and he felt like he was flying. He could barely hold on to the wheel. The world flew by in a blur on either side of him. He was laughing and tears were streaming down his cheeks. "Woo-hoo!" he yelled. "Yeee-haw!" He fucking loved this rocket car.

And then he heard a crack.

In the rear-view mirror, he saw a flash of butter yellow on the track behind him.

The car turned sideways but the momentum was still carrying it forward down the track.

He fumbled around for the parachute button, hitting the dash a few times before getting it right, and then he hit the button — one, two — three times before anything happened.

A giant blossom of white fabric, a snap of his head against the headrest, the screeching of tires. And a long, long terrifying skid to a stop.

A shambling walk back to the start in his ridiculous tight suit.

A wandering harvest of parts and pieces and debris.

And a slow, rattling tow back to the garage.

TRUDY

BECAUSE YOU NEVER KNOW WHAT YOU MIGHT SEE IN THE MOONLIGHT

Trudy had the night off, and Jules said he wanted to make the best of it. They had barbecued burgers and eaten them on the back porch, listening to the crickets and drinking beer. "I have something to show you."

"It had better not be that fucking ramp."

"Nope. It's almost as good, though."

He led her down the steps by the hand. "Come on," he said. "It's a bit of a walk."

They cut across the field behind the house and crossed the highway. Trudy's clothes were already soaked with sweat. Her bare feet rubbed against the insides of her sneakers. "My God," she said. "How far is it?"

"It's worth it," he said. And he led her across another field to a rutted lane lined with trees. As the sun set, bats swooped high above them between the trees, and stars started to blink silver in the dark blue sky. She wanted him to slow down. She hustled up behind him and grabbed at his hand. "Where are we going?"

"Not far now." She planted her feet and pulled him to a stop, shoved him back against a tree and pressed against him, looking into his face. God, he was beautiful. That smile. She kissed him, biting at his lower lip. She ran her hand down over the front of his jeans, squeezing him through the fabric. "Wait," he said.

He nudged her ahead of him down the path and pointed to a break in the trees ahead. They ducked through, thorns catching at their legs. They climbed a low fence and stumbled into a hayfield. She had no idea which direction they were facing any more. "Jesus Christ, Jules. What the hell are we doing?"

He ignored her and kept walking. It was dark now. So dark she couldn't see it until they were almost at the edge. A swimming pool. In the ground. In the middle of a field. She couldn't believe it. It was rectangular, maybe twenty feet long. A row of cement sidewalk around the edge. That was it. No fence, no deck. No house in sight. *What a terrible idea*, she thought, *to put a pool in the middle of a field*. The surface of the water was covered with hay clippings and leaves and milkweed pods. There were probably frogs in there. Crickets were singing in the dark. "Whose is this anyway?"

She looked over at him and he just shrugged. He pulled his shirt over his head, kicked off his shoes and hopped from foot to foot as he took off his jeans and threw them behind him on the prickly cut hay. He stood there, smiling at her, his white skin shining in the moonlight, his hands on his hips, and his erect penis standing out from his body like a tusk. Trudy wondered how many people she knew had ever seen this: a naked man in the moonlight. In all his glory.

Glory.

That word from hymns and anthems. For the first time in her life, Trudy had an inkling of its meaning. She wished she could take a picture of him. Just to look at now and then and remember. She kicked off her shoes. She pulled her T-shirt over her head and took off her bra. She took off her shorts and her underwear and ran toward the pool, leaping in a gangly awkward dive into the water, letting herself sink down to the bottom as the air bubbled out of her nose.

She heard the muffled thump of his body hitting the water, and a few seconds later she felt his hands on her waist and they floated up to the surface together. When they kissed, water ran down their faces, their hair plastered to their foreheads.

Frogs grumbled in the grass all around them, and the silver stars glinted on the surface of the water in tiny white sparks.

BECAUSE NOBODY WILL EVER LOVE YOU ENOUGH

Trudy was lying on her back, staring at the pale blue cracked ceiling of Jules's bedroom. A bare bulb hung from the centre of a bulging round plaster medallion with a snaky braided edge. Their breathing was still heavy, and they were covered in sweat. The electric drone of cicadas came quivering through the open window, but no breeze. Trudy pulled a corner of the sheet just across her hips and turned her head to the side, away from him. She couldn't stop thinking about the jump. Every time it was called off she felt better. Every time it was back on she felt sick. Like a terrible countdown being stopped and started. It was killing her. When she started to speak, her throat felt tight like it was closing. Like her body knew she should not say what she was about to say and was trying to stop her. Her voice sounded thick.

"You can't do it."

Jules was smiling to himself, almost asleep. "What?"

"You cannot do it."

"What are you talking about?"

"The jump. You can't do it. There's no way."

"You better believe I can do it." Jules seemed startled, not quite angry. He pushed himself up on his elbow to look at her.

"No." Trudy could barely push the words out, her throat felt so tight. She was clenching her jaw. "I mean, I don't want you to do it. Don't do it."

"Oh, Trudy. Please. Please don't do this." Trudy knew what he was thinking. *Now this.* The stupid ramp, the stupid car. Another delay. The constant threat of losing his TV deal. And now, this.

Then, out of nowhere, these words came out of Trudy on a wave of salty, bitter tears. And they come out loudly.

"Why?" said Trudy, bunching the sheet in her fists. "Why doesn't anyone ever LOVE ME ENOUGH?" She was out of the bed, grabbing her clothes from the floor, face reddening. Did she mean this? Was it really her true feeling? That nobody ever loved her enough? How pathetic! How embarrassing. She felt so ashamed, she covered her face with her T-shirt. She skidded away from him as he tried to grab her and pull her back into bed. He was talking to her, but she threw her clothes back onto the floor and put her hands over her ears. It was getting silly: he was chasing her around the room now.

She bolted for the door and ran down the hallway. She could hear Jules pivoting to follow her, tripping over himself, as she took a hard left into the bedroom at the end of the hallway. The room that James and Mark shared when they were there. She pushed the door closed and sat on the bed. She was sweating.

The room was dark, the blinds drawn. In most ways it was like Jules's room: dark, rough floorboards, and a high ceiling threaded with cracks. But there was an oriental rug, stained. Brass incense burners and candle holders on every surface. Cowboy boots by a mirror draped with belts and rope. Jules opened the door slowly, the hinges creaking, a smile breaking across his face.

"Fuck off."

Jules laughed. Then he took a running leap and tackled her onto the dark red chenille bedspread. He was tickling her, poking her. He pulled her naked body back against him, put his chin on her shoulder and whispered in her ear.

"Nobody ever loved me enough, either, Trudy. Poor baby." His hand was between her legs now. She laid her head back against his shoulder. "We're just two poor, poor little babies."

BECAUSE THERE IS NO POINT IN LYING

Claire was always lying. That's what Trudy thought. Always. She lied to Mercy, to Trudy, to herself. To her own parents. To everyone at work, everyone she met in town. She lied about how much money they had, how long Tammy had been gone, how soon her lover would return to her. How good their lives were, really. She lied and lied. What was the point? Why bother?

Or she was crying. Lying or crying, one or the other, depending on the day.

Today was a crying day.

There she was when Trudy got home, collapsed in a lawn chair by the back door, head in hands, crying her heart out. It made Trudy feel tired to see her there. It sucked the life out of her. She squeezed her mother's shoulder as she walked past her and into the house. Mercy was kneeling on the couch, a Barbie doll in each fist. She had the dolls facing each other, balanced on their tiptoes on the arm of the couch. She shook them a bit so their hair swung around.

"Grandma's crying again."

"I saw that."

"She says my mum should've come home by now." Mercy bent the Barbies at the hips and seated them on the couch beside her.

Trudy rummaged in her purse for her cigarettes and a lighter. She lit one and blew smoke at the ceiling.

"She says Jules is gonna die. If he does the jump." Mercy waved at the smoke in the air with both hands. "We should stop him and run away. The three of us together. And Grandma Claire, too."

Trudy nodded. Probably. Probably they should stop him from trying to jump the river and run away together.

Mercy was probably right as usual.

BECAUSE YOU THINK YOU'RE SO FUCKING GOOD

Trudy walked across the concrete floor toward her machine in the yellow-green light of the factory. Her head felt as light as a balloon. Her vision was blurry. She had spent too many days with Jules. Too many days arguing and fooling around instead of sleeping. Putting Mercy in front of the TV with her Barbies or leaving her with Mark and James for a couple of hours here and there. Pretending anything could possibly come of it all. Pretending she was someone else from somewhere else living a different kind of life altogether. She could pretend all she wanted, but most nights she still ended up here in this concrete vault, trying not to sew her fingers together.

Dream dissolved. Reality reinstated.

As she got closer to her workstation, she could see that for the third time this week someone had tampered with her machine. It was completely encased, mummified, in white thread. Like a fly in a spider web. Trudy sat down in her chair and stared at it, trying to process how much time, how much patience, must have gone into this endeavour. Winding and winding the thread around the machine — how many times? Hundreds? Thousands?

Lunatics. Fucking morons.

There were murmurs behind her, from the back rows, the cheap seats. It was both amazing and depressing how similar the set-up in the sewing room felt to every classroom she was ever in as a kid. Her, hunched over at the front of the class, trying to focus on her work while listening for a rustle behind her, waiting for something to sail through the air and hit her in the back of the head. She picked up her scissors and started cutting through the thread. She had to cut through one thin layer at a time. It made a tearing sound as the blades worked their way through. Like the sound of cutting through bandages.

Trudy knew why she was being harassed. She was being punished for the number one small-town crime: Thinking You're Good. As in: *You think you're good, don't you?* Everybody knew that she had put her name in for the dayshift. Another fantasy. Another case of Trudy thinking she was *good*. But she knew she didn't have a chance. She didn't have the seniority, wasn't productive enough, was always causing trouble. And then there was Mercy. Even with school starting in September, Trudy and Claire both working days would leave Mercy home alone for two hours or more. It could never work.

At the end of her shift, as Trudy was punching out, Jeannie appeared beside her. "How's your bullshit boyfriend, Trudy?"

"Shut up, Jeannie."

"Thinks he's something special, eh? Thinks he's Superman or something. Looks like a fucking loser to me."

"You would know."

"Because you're so much better, right, Trudy?"

There it was. *You think you're good, don't you, Trudy?*

"Yup."

"Because what?" Jeannie had followed her out to the parking lot, the late summer sun making the asphalt slightly soft under their shoes. Trudy kept walking, looking straight ahead. She could see her car at the end of the lot. It had been wrapped in toilet paper, streamers of it fluttering in the breeze. And someone had upended a garbage can onto the hood, its former contents scattered on and around her car: a browning apple core, a used Maxi pad, some crumpled up foil, banana peels, and pop cans.

"Why, Trudy? Why do you think you're so much better than the rest of us? Wait. Let me guess. Is it your job? No, that can't be right." Jeannie feigned confusion, looking up at the sky, tilting her head to the side.

"Fuck off, Jeannie." Trudy kept walking.

"Is it your fancy clothes, your nice house? No, can't be that . . . your high level of education? Nope, not that either." Jeannie threw her foot out to the side, kicking Trudy's shin so that she tripped and lurched forward. Trudy turned her head to the side as she fell to save her face and her bare shoulder skidded painfully across the pavement.

"Oops! Sorry, Trudy!" Jeannie turned to walk away, but Trudy lunged across the pavement to grab her by the ankles. Jeannie pitched forward onto the ground, flat on her chest, the air knocked out of her lungs with a thud, a percussive *hoof* issuing from her mouth. Trudy was on her now, sitting on her back, using both hands to pin Jeannie's wrists to the ground. *Here we go again*, she thought. She suddenly felt very tired. Her body felt like lead. She grabbed a handful of Jeannie's coarse rusty hair in her fist and yanked her head back. She bent down, her face beside Jeannie's cheek.

"Jeannie, please just fuck off. Or I will kill you." Jeannie was silent, glaring sideways at her. "I don't know why you even give a shit what I think, Jeannie. Why do you care?" She let go of her hair. "Just leave me alone, OK?"

As Trudy got up and walked toward her car, Jeannie rolled onto her back. When she finally caught her breath, she sat up and yelled, "*Cunt!*"

Trudy did not turn around; she let this pass through her. Oh, Jeannie and her clever *repartee*.

She opened her car door and got in. She turned on the wipers, which cleared enough paper away so that she could see out of the windshield. She backed up fast so that the garbage can slid off the front of the hood. She couldn't really see out the back window, but she didn't care if there was anything or anyone behind her. Then she put it in drive and peeled away.

PART 2

SO LONG AT THE FAIR

BECAUSE THE END OF SUMMER MEANS
THE BEGINNING OF SOMETHING ELSE

Mercy loves parades. She loves to see the tractors pulling the floats, the beauty queens, the horses, the marching girls in their uniforms sending their batons whirling into the air. The spray of candy flying off the backs of trailers, kids scrambling along the side of the road, filling their pockets. It is Old Home Week in Preston Mills. This means several things. It means boring things like tractor pulls and church lunches that take forever, where Mercy will dutifully eat soft carrots and green beans and sit still for hours without complaining. But it also means the fair, fireworks, and, tomorrow, a parade.

Old Home Week also means the end of summer. It means that soon she will get to go to school.

"Grandma Claire, can I go on the Tilt-a-Whirl?" Mercy and Claire are walking along the packed-dirt path of the midway, picking at giant puffs of gauzy pink cotton candy. Speckles shuffles along beside them, the leash hanging slack from Claire's wrist. Trudy has gone off to find Jules, who is doing a rocket car "demonstration" somewhere on the edge of the fairground.

"Maybe later, hon. How about the Merry-Go-Round?"

"That's for babies!"

"Ferris wheel?"

"OK. But later maybe we can go on the Tilt-a-Whirl?"

"Maybe."

BECAUSE WHAT GOES UP MUST COME DOWN

Claire looks over at the Tilt-a-Whirl, the giant laughing clown head in the middle of the track, the cars wheeling around and up and down, thumps and screams escaping from underneath the metal canopies. She steers her charges toward the Ferris wheel, looking doubtfully at the attendant leaning against the fence. He is shirtless and tanned a deep red-brown. When he smiles, his teeth are very close to the same colour as his skin. The colour of baked beans, thinks Claire.

"Two please!" Mercy hands him the tickets as Claire loops the leash around the fence. Speckles howls after them as they get on the ride. The attendant puts the bar down in front of them, which touches Claire's belly but looks to be about six inches from Mercy. Claire puts her arm around the little girl and pulls her close. She closes her eyes as they rise up, up into the air, the metal of the contraption screeching. "Grandma! I can't breathe!"

"Sorry, hon." Claire eases her grip on Mercy, opens her eyes, and looks with wonder across the fairground. She sees the other rides, the tops of the chip trucks, the tops of peoples' heads in groups here and there, and to the left of it all, the wide grey rippling St. Lawrence River. "Oh, Mercy. Look at that."

Mercy is leaning across her grandmother's lap, her hair blowing around, getting into Claire's eyes and nose. "Jules is gonna jump right over that whole thing. He is gonna fly, Grandma Claire!"

Oh, I hope not, thinks Claire. *Surely not.*

Mercy spreads her arms wide like wings as they drop over the crest of the wheel and begin their descent.

BECAUSE THERE ARE RUDE SURPRISES IN THIS LIFE

The car is pulled over onto the gravel shoulder of the road. Trudy is behind the wheel, fuming. Jules is staring out the passenger side, his left eye blackened and slowly swelling shut. His hair stands up in a plume at the back of his head. His clothes are covered in dirt. Mercy is crying. And Claire, poor Claire, is bent over, throwing up into the ditch beside the road. Mercy scrambles out of the car and starts patting Claire's back.

"I'm sorry, Grandma. I didn't know it would be like that." This is true. Mercy thought the Tilt-a-Whirl would be fun. Gentle. A slightly more exciting version of the Merry-Go-Round.

But no.

The minute it had started, she had been terrified. The ride lurched into motion and Mercy smacked her head against the back of the car. It swung this way and then that, it went up and down. She couldn't tell which way it would go next. It threw them around, Mercy's jeans sliding across the slippery seat. One minute she was on top of Grandma Claire; the next, Grandma Claire was crushing her against the side. Mercy had been sure they would be thrown right off the ride. She started to yell at the operator every time she could see him, *Stop the ride! STOP THE RIDE!*

Mercy's yelling had started within the first full rotation of the ride, around ten seconds in; but it just went on. And on. It swung and it lurched. It tilted and whirled. Both Mercy and Claire had found themselves praying for death.

Claire coughs. Another volley of hot pink vomit splatters onto the grass in front of her feet. Mercy takes a step back.

"Grandma Claire, I didn't know."

"I knew."

"What?"

"I knew what it would be like! That's why I didn't want to go on it! But you wouldn't stop, Mercy. Tilt-a-Whirl this! Tilt-a-Whirl that! Well, you got your *Tilt-a-Whirl*, didn't you?" Claire digs in her purse for a tissue, wipes her mouth, and heads back to the car. Mercy follows.

"I didn't like it either." Mercy is squinting up at the sky. "I thought I would. But I didn't."

Claire grunts. Rolls her eyes. They settle into the back seat.

"Are you mad at me, Grandma Claire?"

"No."

"I'm sorry. I'm really sorry I even had that idea. It was a bad idea." She shakes her head and looks out the window. This day at the fair hadn't turned out the way she thought it would.

Sometimes it's like that.

BECAUSE SOMETIMES IT'S BETTER TO JUST TURN AROUND AND WALK AWAY

Jules's day at the fair hadn't gone the way he thought it would, either.

When he showed up at the fairground, a crowd was already gathering around the edges of the field. Great! The bleachers were full. His plan was to do a short jump (a half-dozen junkyard cars between two wooden ramps), start up the show car — let it shoot some flames and sparks out of its back end — and then shake some hands. Strictly routine. Nothing fancy. He didn't want to risk getting hurt again before the main event. The new date — now the third date — for the jump was less than a month away, if all went well. He had his jumpsuit on with the red maple leaves down the sides. Calm, cool, and collected.

And then that ferret Sammy Harrison came scampering over. Big smile on his face. It seemed to Jules that Sammy was at his most cheerful when delivering bad news.

"I wouldn't go over there if I were you."

"What?"

"People are pretty pissed off, Jules. It might be better just to lay low for a while."

"What are you talking about?"

Jules strained to look around Sammy's giant blond head at the crowd milling around in the distance. Were they holding signs?

"Let's go, Jules."

Would it have been better to stop then? To turn around, walk back to his car, and go home? To spare himself this glimpse into the black heart of Preston Mills? Jules would never know. Because he did not turn around and walk away. What he did was push Sammy out of the way and walk over to the field as if everything were perfectly normal. Business as usual.

As he approached the crowd, people grew quiet. His pace slowed as he looked up at the bleachers and saw about fifty men, women, and children looking at him with disgust. They held signs with slogans. Variations on a theme. JULES TREMBLAY IS A CHICKEN or, simply, CHICKENSHIT! or TREMBLAY: JUMP OR DIE! There was a subcategory, as well, that focused on his being French-Canadian: AU REVOIR, JULES! (He was impressed by this.) And, less kindly: DIE, FROG! A chant started . . . *Jump.*

Jump.

JUMP!

JUMP!   *JUMP!*   *JUMP!*

Jules thought maybe he could turn it around. A few jokes, a reassuring story. A reminder that he was real, human, like them. That he meant to jump. That it wasn't his fault the jump had been delayed. Twice. He was not tricking them. He raised his hand above his head to get their attention. Then something sailed through the air, shining red. A candy apple hit him in the forehead, sending him back on his heels, almost knocking him over. A streak of bright red shone above his right eyebrow. Then a shower of debris followed: popcorn cartons, ice cream cones, apple cores. As he started backing away, he looked over at the show car and saw that all the windows had been broken and the tires slashed.

Not knowing what else to do, he turned his back on the crowd and started to walk away. He saw Trudy coming toward him from the edge of the field, ducking, her hand shielding her face from being pelted with garbage.

Jules heard the scrape of boots on dirt behind him. As he turned, he saw the smiling blockheaded face of Jimmy Munro.

He saw a fat, clenched fist.

Three bright flashes of light accompanied by a whirring sound.

Whirr–whirr–whirr.

A fluttering, dusky gloom filled his eyes.

Then pure black.

BECAUSE JOY CAN FILL YOU UP AND
SEND YOU RIGHT UP INTO THE SKY

And just like that, summer is over.

"Don't worry, Mercy. It's going to be OK." Trudy is staring straight ahead, watching the road. How can she stand it? Mercy going to school. It is unspeakable. *Well*, she thinks, *at least Jules is still around*. Small mercies: the summer has come and gone and her boyfriend had not driven his car off a ramp into the river. Yet. Every time Trudy drives past the ramp, she glares at it, hoping to bring it crashing to the ground with her mind. It is not out of the question. One day, she saw a hunk of earth the size of a tractor-trailer just crumble off one side and go land-sliding across the field in pieces.

She fiddles with the radio to see if she can find a good song. "Joy to the World" is playing. She can live with that. Joy to the fishes and the bullfrogs and all that.

"It's going to be great!" Mercy shouts over the music. She loves this song. She is bouncing a little in her seat, looking out the window. "When will we get there? This drive is long."

"Don't let anybody push you around." Trudy is feeling a little sick, shaky. It hadn't hit her until this morning. This dread. She wishes she could keep Mercy at home with her and Claire forever.

"Nobody's gonna be mean to me, Trudy. We're all going to be friends." She turns to address her directly, to make sure she is listening. "They're all just little kids like me, Trudy." Mercy looks out the window again and sighs. "I wish Speckles could come to school. Why can't dogs come to school with you, Trudy?"

Trudy ignores the question, keeps driving. She is thinking about how, when she was in school, there were some kids who had terrified her, who had made every single day a trial. Mostly boys, but some girls, too. Kids who, if you said hello to them, would laugh in your face. But if you walked by without saying hello, they would deride you for being a snob, for being *too good*. They would trip you as you walked by or shove your shoulder so that you fell sideways. Kids who would love an excuse, any excuse at all, to punch you right in the face.

She hadn't realized until halfway through high school that she had developed a sort of system, an actual physical posture of avoidance. Rolling her shoulders forward so her chest would not stick out, hands in pockets, tucking her buttocks in. Staring at the ground or to the side when she passed people. Making herself smaller, quieter. Like a sad old beaten-up dog.

It is too much.

How can she let Mercy go, just to be swallowed up by it all? It doesn't seem right. It doesn't seem possible that there is no choice. That there is only one way for kids to grow up. But the car is parked now and her feet keep walking across the pavement. One foot in front of the other.

They walk across the parking lot to the kindergarten playground, holding hands. Mercy is hopping on one foot. She looks so happy, like she can barely stay tethered to the ground. The morning air is just a little bit cool, and the white sun flashes through the leaves of the trees around the grassy yard. It is early and there are a few kids — maybe half a dozen — milling around. Mercy lets go of Trudy's hand and runs across the grass. Trudy watches her as she stops and talks to one kid, then another, then another.

Mercy pirouettes around them, her fine straight hair flying around in the breeze.

She turns and looks back at Trudy for a moment, checking to see if she is still there.

Trudy waves but stays where she is. Breathing. She looks down at her feet on the pavement. Tanned nut-brown in her Jesus sandals, the grass of the yard just past her big toes.

When she looks up again, Mercy is standing face to face with another girl. They hold each other by both hands, their foreheads almost touching. Mercy is smiling with her head cocked to one side. Her knees are bent, sprung tight, like she is about to leap into the air.

Like she is about to launch herself high into the pale blue morning sky.

BECAUSE YOU DON'T ALWAYS WANT
TO HEAR WHAT OTHER PEOPLE THINK

Jules is meeting his hero.

Lionel "Lightning" Jones. The world's most famous daredevil. In his star-spangled leather jumpsuits and capes, he has jumped over cars, school busses, waterfalls, and canyons on his motorcycle. He has thick blond hair, a Pepsodent smile, and claims to have broken every bone in his body at least once. And the network has sent him to Preston Mills, Ontario, to look at the site of The Mile Jump.

The cameras are rolling. Jules is sweating, baking in the heat of the September sun. Finally, some dry weather. Better late than never. Lightning Jones looks out over the end of the ramp, then down at his feet.

"When's the jump?"

"September twenty-third. Ten days away!" Jules tries for a smile, thinks he might make some kind of joke, but nothing comes to him. His throat hurts. Lightning turns away from him, squints into the sunlight.

"Shouldn't the ground settle or something? Didn't they just finish this thing?"

"It's fine. Totally fine. That's what they tell me, anyway." Jules laughs unconvincingly, clears his throat. "It has to be." Only that last syllable doesn't quite make it out. His voice stops abruptly. His throat is closing, Jules is sure of it. The camera swings back toward Lightning.

"Sure looks like a dangerous jump to me, boy. If you land in that water, you better have someone to get you out quick." He shakes his head and puts his hand on Jules's shoulder. "I wouldn't do it. No, sir."

Whump, whump, whump. Jules can hear his own heartbeat, and something shadowy darts at the outside edge of his vision. The air seems to hum around his head.

Lightning pats Jules twice on the shoulder and turns on his big wide smile for the camera. "You never know. Could be the daredevil stunt to end them all, buddy!"

The cameraman nods, takes the camera off his shoulder, and starts packing up. Lightning reaches out and shakes Jules's hand. He shrugs and turns to walk away down the ramp. Jules turns to follow him and almost trips. Pins and needles shoot up his leg. His foot has fallen asleep. Goddamn thing. Always doing that these days.

Two days later, Sammy calls to say the network thinks the jump is too risky to broadcast live.

Jules is pretty sure he knows what that means.

BECAUSE SOME RIDES ARE TOO ROUGH

Jules has driven for three and a half hours to see his roommates in a small-town rodeo. Trudy declined to accompany him.

Mark has successfully ridden two bulls, both of them heavy and sluggish but just energetic enough to earn him some points and keep him in the game. Both times he ended his ride by neatly jumping off and landing on his feet. One more and it will have been worth it to come. The next one will not be so easy, though. Mark casts a glance at the bull in the chute.

The bull's name is Frankincense and Murder, son of Frankenbull, grandson of Frankenstein's Monster. So it goes. Generation after generation of thundering evil. The bull swings its head toward the clutch of cowboys behind him. Its eyes bulge so that a ring of white shows at the edges.

Jules watches as Mark lowers himself onto the back of the bull, his legs spread wide, straining. He shimmies forward until his crotch is touching the rope that is wrapped once around the huge chest of the animal, behind its shoulders. James is standing beside him on a rung of the fence, pulling the rope tight. A third cowboy stands on top of the fence on the other side with one boot on the shoulder of the bull, trying to push it away from the side of the pen. The bull is the colour of wet sand and weighs about eighteen hundred pounds. Muscles ripple below its coarse-haired hide.

Jules wonders again: *Why do we do these things? What has brought us here?*

Mark's gloved hand is palm up on the back of the bull, flattened under the first round of rope. James gives the rope another heave straight up, and then Mark grabs it and wraps it around his hand twice. He has to use his other hand to bend his fingers closed around it. The bull shifts against the side of the pen, pinning Mark's leg. Slowly, the bull increases force until Mark is wincing with pain. The bull kicks the back of the pen and then crouches down, kneeling forward, unseating the cowboy.

Fuck.

Mark unwraps the rope and is lifted off. They will have to start all over again.

For the first time, Jules thinks his friend looks like he is getting nervous.

It starts to rain. The arena is turning to mud. Eight seconds is all Mark needs. Stay on the bull for eight seconds. Get to the final round. Win a thousand bucks. Drive home. *Please. Jesus,* thinks Jules. *Just one more time.*

They start the procedure again. Mark sits astride the bull, shimmies forward. The rope is wrapped around the animal and pulled tight, then around the cowboy's hand and pulled tight again. Gloved hand folded over rope. Hat crushed down on head. A quick nod and the gate is thrown open.

Jules has a bad feeling. He doesn't want to watch. But he has to watch.

The bull explodes out of the chute like it has been shot out of a cannon. It leaps skyward, throwing its hips up and kicking out the back. Mark is sticking to it, one hand in the air. The bull spins to the right, bucking. All four hooves are off the ground at once, the bull twisting its body in midair, trying to send the cowboy flying off over its backside. No dice. Mark is still there, knees driven into the sides of the animal, bending at the waist, keeping that hand high.

Two seconds left before the horn blows.

The bull throws its weight into another spin, bucking, reaching a horn back, trying to catch the cowboy's leg. Then one huge leap upward. Mark pulls his torso up straight, his whole body is tensed, waiting for the bull's front hooves to hit the ground, sending its ass high into the air. Mark leans back, anticipating. But the bull slips in the mud, slides to the side, sending Mark flying through the air.

The horn sounds before he hits the ground. It counts! The ride counts! Jules is elated. Sends a fist skyward.

Except Mark hits the ground headfirst.

His body bends at the waist then flops over onto the ground like a rag doll.

Four clowns appear out of nowhere, all suspenders and baggy shorts. They circle the bull; they clap, they hoot and holler, wave hats in the bull's face, dance backward toward the break in the fence. Leading the bull away.

Away from the still, still figure on the ground.

Jules turns his back and covers his face with both hands.

BECAUSE SOMETIMES YOU JUST WANT TO GO HOME

Fenton has a bad feeling. He is standing outside the back door, his hand on the doorknob, gathering his strength. He listens.

Nothing.

Not a sound.

He takes a deep breath and opens the door into the kitchen. Tammy is not there.

The table is gleaming clean. The chairs are pushed in. The floor has been swept and mopped. He removes his boots and places them on the mat, as he has been told to do hundreds, possibly thousands, of times. He is not always good at remembering things. He pads across the kitchen to the living room. Tammy is not there, either.

He looks down the hallway and sees that the bathroom door is closed. But there is no sound. He steps closer, creeping as quietly as he can. He places his ear against the door. The sound of water dripping into a full tub, a ripple of movement in the water.

A quiet moan, a sniff.

Fenton draws back from the door, spooked. "Tammy?"

No answer.

"Tammy, you OK?" Fenton is scared now. He feels like a child, standing there in his sock feet in the hallway.

"Just come in, Fenton." He barely hears it. She says: "Just come in already."

Fenton opens the door cautiously, as though something might spring out at him. Nothing about this feels right. He looks in to see Tammy, beautiful Tammy, lying in the bath. Her head, her nipples, and her knees are the only parts of her above the water line, like little islands scattered across the surface. The air is warm and humid, making his shirt cling to his chest. Fenton is not usually allowed into the bathroom when Tammy is in the bath. He is not usually allowed to see her naked in the daylight anymore. Not since she told him to stop coming to the bar. She is the most beautiful thing he has ever seen. And then there is another surprise: she looks at him with love in her eyes. And tears.

Now he is truly afraid.

"Honey, what's wrong?"

"I love you, Fenton."

This can't be good, he thinks. "Jesus Christ." Fenton sits on the lid of the toilet. He looks at his feet. Prays to stay conscious, not to succumb to the strangeness that can overtake him sometimes. He wants to see everything, hear everything. Something important is happening.

Tammy laughs. She wipes her eyes. "Come on in here, babe. There's room." She sits up to make space for him at the drain end of the tub. Fenton takes off his socks and unbuckles his belt, drops his pants to the floor. Tammy is still smiling at him and tears are running down her cheeks. He pulls his shirt off and dips a toe into the hot water. He eases himself in and the water threatens to overflow. They are careful not to slosh around too much as they find a way to make all four of their legs fit together comfortably. Fenton has to sit to the side to avoid the faucet. His neck hurts as he looks at her beautiful face. "What's going on?"

A sob like a shout comes out of her and startles him. He holds her feet in his hands under the water. She shakes her head. "I want to go home, Fenton. I want to see my baby."

She is weeping now, gasping for air. Fenton strains forward to reach her, to take her in his arms, but he can only reach around her bent knees. He pulls himself up, using the sides of the tub. He splashes around noisily, awkwardly rearranging himself until he is kneeling between her legs. Water splashes over the edge of the tub and onto the floor as he reaches down and pries her away from the back of the tub. He pulls her slippery shuddering body close and waits.

He just holds her and waits until she tells him what to do next.

BECAUSE THE SUN ON THE WATER
LOOKS LIKE DIAMONDS

Tammy is driving like a fucking lunatic. She is heading east on Highway 2 and Fenton is hanging out the window like a big, skinny, happy dog. She takes the curves sharp and at speed as the sunlit trees fly by the driver's side window in a brilliant haze, the wide blue river winding in and out of view on the right. *Some highway!* So narrow it is barely wide enough for two cars, trees encroaching from either side, making a tunnel to shoot through in the cool sunlight. So many curves and dips you'd have to be crazy to pass anybody. (Which she is, and she does.) Towns so small, so indistinguishable from the miles of fields and forests between them, only the green-and-white road signs attest to their existence: Johnstown, Cardinal, Iroquois.

Blink and you'll miss them, thinks Fenton.

Tammy takes another curve and looks over, smiling at him, her hair flying around her face. Cigarette packs and matches and wadded up foil burger wrappers slide across the bench seat and settle against his thigh.

"Light me a smoke, Fenton!"

Fenton hunches forward and pushes the lighter in, checks two empty packs and tosses them on the floor, then fishes a cigarette out of a third. He bobbles it as Tammy flies over a sharp little rise in the road and his ass leaves the seat for a second.

"Jesus, woman! Slow down!" he says, but he is laughing. He loves it when she is happy.

He lights the cigarette and takes a long drag before handing it across to her. He blows the smoke out the window and looks out at the ripples on the water. *Diamonds*, he thinks. The sun on the water always looks like diamonds. No other way to describe it. And as he looks at the water, it recedes a bit, like a photograph being pulled away across the flat surface of a table.

BECAUSE A TUMOUR IS THE LAST THING YOU NEED

Tammy can see him starting to slump in his seat out of the corner of her eye. She shoves at his shoulder.

"Fenton! *Earth calling!*"

He tries to stay with her, but he can't. His eyes close and his head falls forward and to the side.

Tammy steps on it, then turns onto a gravel road, the back of the truck fishtailing behind them. She pulls to a stop at the end of the road. There is a graveyard to the left, the rocky shore and the river straight ahead, trees on the right reaching over top of the road and touching above the truck. *Tunnel of love*, she thinks. She lifts Fenton's chin and turns his face toward her. He opens his eyes. Then closes them. He mumbles something that sounds like *Sorry*.

"*Sorry?* You better be sorry. You son of a bitch, Fenton. You better not have a fucking *brain tumour*. That's all I need." These episodes of Fenton's are starting to scare her. She leans back in her seat, looks out at the glittering surface of the water.

"I'm here," says Fenton. "I'm right here." His eyes are still closed, and his hands are trembling a little, vibrating against the seat. Tammy slides over close to him, sweeps the garbage off the seat and onto the floor. She ducks her head so she doesn't bump it on the ceiling as she straddles his lap. She pulls off her top and takes off her bra. Then she lifts up his T-shirt, pushes her bare breasts against him, and starts gently kissing his lips.

She kisses his mouth over and over again until he starts kissing her back.

BECAUSE SUNDAY IS THE LORD'S DAY (NOT YOURS)

It is Sunday. Darren Robertson's forty-fifth birthday. Forty-five! How the hell did that happen? He hadn't slept all night. At the kitchen sink, washing the breakfast dishes, he looks out over the backyard. It looks like he feels: shitty and busted up. There are groundhog holes, more dandelions and thistles than grass, a wooden fence that has buckled and caved in at the northwest corner, possibly home to a nest of rabbits. The yard is a fucking disgrace.

Pulling off his yellow rubber gloves with a snap, he thinks, *Yes. Today is the day.*

He is going to get out there and make something of that crappy yard. Clean it up. Fix the fence. Maybe pull up a patch of sod in the back corner so he can plant a vegetable garden next year. Maybe he can even set up a little fountain.

As a rule, Darren tries not to think about them. But every year on his birthday, he thinks about the girls. How old they would be: Trudy would be twenty-three this year, he guesses, and Tammy would be twenty-two. He thinks about how they must have their own adult lives now. How they must hate him. How they are right to hate him. And he tries not to think about Claire. Oh, the mess he made.

So many messes a single human man can make in forty-five years. So many and so large.

Darren heads out to the yard in his old jeans and rubber boots. He is already too hot, sweating inside his flannel shirt. He digs up the massive weeds one by one with a spade, shakes the soil off the roots, and flings them over the fence. Hour after hour, weed after weed, working in tight rows, back and forth across the lawn. He looks back at what he has done. It looks worse than ever: brown divots all over the place. He is not sure whether it is better to stop or to keep going. The sun is warm now, high overhead, and he has a tight feeling in his chest every time he breathes. Like he might hiccup or belch.

But nothing happens.

Just this feeling like a knot tightening deep inside his chest.

Then he thinks he sees something sparkling in the sunlight in the hole he has just dug, but he can't see what it is. He sees a worm slide out of the dark earth and back in. Light bounces off something at the bottom of the hole again. What *is* it?

Darren tries to kneel to get a closer look but falls forward and onto his side. The side of his face is on the grass. It smells like summer and fall all at once: grass and soil and dried leaves. Pain fills his chest and freezes him in place. It spreads up to his jaw, makes him close his eyes. He makes a sound like an old cow lowing, begging to be milked.

Mmmmmuh-AAAW!

Starting to feel desperate now, he thinks of Michelle in the house somewhere. Maybe talking on the phone, maybe watching church on TV. He is struggling to open his eyes, to make a louder sound, to send a signal to his wife inside the house. To beam a message to her with his mind: *HELP ME!*

But his eyes stay closed. No sound comes out of his mouth. His brain sends no signal.

Today is the day, he thinks. *Today I will die.*

Forty-five years is all you get, Darren Robertson. You busted-up mess. You dug-up yard full of holes. Today is the Lord's Day.

Not yours.

BECAUSE THE HOSPITAL IS NEVER FUN FOR LONG

Darren opens his eyes and sees the ceiling, the fluorescent lights of the hospital scrolling by overhead. He hears footsteps and rustling and someone saying his name. Then he hears nothing, sees nothing. Black, blue, yellow sparks of light shimmer behind his eyelids. He is out, gone again. *One . . . two . . . three . . . four . . .* and then there it is again: the white ceiling, the rectangles of light rolling by like the cars of a train.

OK, now, someone says. A stranger. It is a stranger's voice that says: *OK now, Mr. Robertson. Just relax.* And he does. Like magic. He lets the head inside his head fall back onto the pillow and the body inside his body sink down into the mattress, and he watches as the corridors just keep wheeling by as if there were no end to anything at all. As if all of eternity were a bed rolling down hospital corridors with the bright ceiling floating above, white as a nurse's cap.

They take his blood. They listen to his heart. They check his blood pressure. They say quiet, soothing words. A nurse lays her hand on his shoulder. They give him some medicine. He falls asleep.

When he wakes up again, nobody is there. Or, at least, nobody *upright* is there. Three other men, lying on their backs, hooked up to monitors are there with him. It is nighttime and the windows are blue. A pale blue curtain hangs near his bed. There is a humming sound and the occasional rattle of a cart in the hallway. Everything looks blue and moonlit. What peace! Just this quiet ticking and humming and the gentle blue light of the hospital at night.

I could stay here forever, he thinks.

Until his faculties return and he begins to feel things.

His mouth is dry. His shoulder is sore. His skin is hot. His ribs ache like he has been punched. He wants to feel like he did just a few minutes earlier.

Light. Empty. Absent.

Now he feels like old meat and bones on a hard bed. In a strange room in the middle of the night. Alone.

The doctor drops by to tell him that he has been a fool. These aren't his exact words of course. The doctor tells Darren a number of things. No, he has not had a heart attack. Yes, they are certain. No, there doesn't seem to be anything else wrong. No, his wife was not there. She has not called. Yes, he can go home. There is no need for him to stay any longer.

The doctor also asks Darren a number of questions that don't sit well with him. Has he been sleeping well? (No, though he never has.) Has he been worried? Has he been drinking more than usual? (Yes, but that's nothing new, either, and No.) The doctor nods. Smiles a little. Pats the bed briskly and gets up. Tells him not to worry. To get more fresh air and exercise. And to tell his wife not to call the ambulance next time.

Just nerves. Fatigue. Wear and tear. Nothing serious.

(Shitty. Old. Busted up. Nuisance.)

As the doctor disappears through the blue curtains, Darren pulls his rickety, foggy, humiliated self out of the bed and looks around for his clothes. He pulls them on, rubs his eyes, and shambles down the corridor to reception. The nurse calls Michelle twice. No answer. They shrug at each other with half a smile. She takes a call and swivels in her chair. He turns away and heads out into the night, cuts across the parking lot toward home.

BECAUSE THE NEW DAY IS PINK

And sure enough, Darren's wife is gone. Somehow he knew she would be. He has a pretty good idea where she has gone. And with whom. Her car is gone. Her dresser drawers are empty. Half the cutlery is gone. Exactly half the dishes. Half the glasses and pots and pans. He finds this precision surprising. Out of character. His laundry has been done. Folded and put away. (This he finds truly shocking. In over twenty-five years of marriage, this has never happened.) She has left the stereo and all the records, thank God, but has taken the big console TV. There is a deep rectangular outline in the rug where it used to sit, looming over the living room. She must have had help with that.

Darren puts Steve Miller Band on the turntable, lowers the needle, and adjusts the volume. He stares at the soaring white horse with rainbow wings on the cover and smiles. *Book of Dreams.* He sits on the couch in the dark, the streetlight shining in through the bay window, and wonders how to feel. More accurately, he wonders if he should wonder how to feel. Or if he should just accept this beautiful, gradual deflation he feels inside his chest. This rolling back of the dark clouds in his head.

It has been clear to him for a long time now that it is possible to love somebody and at the same time know that if this person just, say, *evaporated* one day, just disappeared into thin air, your life would be thousands of times better. That was the simple truth. He doesn't think it is quite the same as wishing someone dead. That would be too complicated. Too fraught. He had, however, wished her gone. And now she was.

He takes his clothes off slowly. They are grass-stained from the yard, clammy from the hospital, and cold from the walk home. It is a relief to have them off. He leaves them there on the carpet in a pile, underwear on top, and heads down the hallway to the kitchen. He stands naked at the sink and looks out the window at the dimpled yard. His handiwork. The sun is coming up, tinting the air all rosy gold. *It is a new pink day,* thinks Darren as the sun angles in through the window and his tears splash noisily, one by one, into the stainless-steel sink. They sound like this when they fall:

Pink! *Pink!* *Pink!* *Pink!*

THE CIRCUS

BECAUSE YOU THINK YOU KNOW WHAT YOU'RE IN FOR

"A truck is here!" Mercy calls to Trudy from the bottom of the stairs. The dog is barking and whining. *Trudy! A truck is here!*

Trudy flips her pillow over and lays her cheek on the cool cotton of the pillowcase. She closes her eyes again and starts to fade. It is late afternoon, and she has been trying to get to sleep. Just a quick nap before Claire returns and dinner gets made and she has to go to work and the whole damn thing starts all over again.

"TRUDY! I THINK IT'S MY MOM!" At this, Trudy sits bolt upright. Really? *Come on.* Mercy thunders up the stairs, Speckles in tow, and stands wild-eyed at the bedroom door. "Trudy, I'm worried."

Trudy pulls a T-shirt on over her undershirt, grabs a pair of jeans. "Just give me a second, hon, and we'll go see who it is together. Stay right there."

Trudy fights her way into her jeans, trying to listen for the sound of a car door slamming or the front door opening. She heads for the stairs. Mercy can't help it — she is following too close and she steps on the heel of Trudy's moccasin.

"Mercy!" Trudy catapults forward, saving herself just before the top of the stairs. "Jesus."

"Sorry!"

Trudy pushes Speckles back behind her with her foot flat against the dog's wrinkled brow and takes Mercy's hand. The three of them bump and tussle down the stairs. Trudy pulls the front curtain back and, sure enough, sees her sister in the driver's seat of an old beat-up turquoise truck. Making out with some guy. Classic.

"Wait here, Mercy. I just need to check something." And she heads for the door.

"Wait, Trudy!" Mercy is standing on the couch again. Bouncing. Speckles is whining and squirming and wagging her tail.

"I'll just be a minute, hon." *Just long enough to stave her head in with a shovel*, she thinks.

"But, Trudy, wait! There's *another truck*!"

BECAUSE NOBODY INVITED YOU

Trudy is not having a good week. As she looks through the screen door at her sister — her sister who is laughing, pushing her now-blond hair back from her beautiful face — Trudy wonders again how much she is expected to take in this life. Just how much exactly?

Only a week ago, she had been lying in bed, curled around Jules's back. His skin was warm, sweet-smelling. She had laid her cheek against his back and held him tight against her. The house was cold, and they had piled so many blankets on top of them, they could barely move. It was like a soft muffled cave-world under there. She wished she could stay there forever. For the thousandth time, she wondered what her life would be like if she could just work in the daylight and sleep at night. If she didn't have to haul herself out of bed just as everybody else was settling in for the night.

When she woke again, the house was dark and she could hear Jules talking in another room. The clock said 8:30. Trudy sat up and reached for her cigarettes, listening, trying to make out what he was saying, but she could only hear the odd mumbled syllable. Then it was just quiet. She pulled a blanket around her shoulders and walked as quietly as she could down the hall to the kitchen.

Jules was sitting in a chair, receiver to ear, forehead on the table. Listening. Trudy stood in the doorway and watched him and waited. When he finally spoke again, it was if he were using someone else's voice. Or, at least, one she hadn't heard before: he was speaking French. She couldn't understand a word. Well, she did understand one word. Near the end of the conversation she thought she heard him say that something — or everything — was *fucké*.

That seemed clear enough.

She pulled the edges of the blanket up off the floor and crept back to the bedroom where she lay down and pretended to sleep. It felt cold without him there. She stretched her legs across to his side of the bed to see if there was any residual warmth where he had lain beside her all afternoon. Nothing. It was cold as stone.

"I have to go away for a few days," he said.

"I'll be back before you know it," he said.

Seven days ago, he had said this. And not a word since.

Before he left, he had kissed her forehead and not her mouth. Not her ear or her neck or her shoulder. He had pulled her toward him and placed a dry little kiss on her forehead. Like a tired old man.

And the day after he left, Mercy turned five. It had been a small party. The usual suspects, the constant three: Trudy, Claire, and Mercy. And Speckles, of course. No Jules. And certainly no Tammy. Claire had made a heart-shaped cake, and Trudy had picked up pizza. Pepperoni, as requested. Just two high, thin voices singing "Happy Birthday," and a deep howl from the dog. Trudy found it so sad.

But not Mercy. She was wriggling in her chair, ready to blow out her candles, full of bright, earnest wishes.

Maybe a wish had come true. Maybe Mercy had brought Tammy back.

They are not the guests Trudy would have chosen, but here they are anyway.

BECAUSE TIME TRAVELS IN BOTH DIRECTIONS

Oh, the roads are like ribbons. This was the thought that went through Darren's mind as he drove hour after hour, all the way from Brownsville to Preston Mills. *The roads are just like skeins of ribbon unwinding before me and behind me.* Even though it had been twenty years, it was effortless, this long drive back. All day long, his heart fluttered like a little bird in his chest, and the truck glided along the roads like a bead on a string. Home, home. He would go back to the place where he had left her, and if his luck was very good, he would find her again.

(And if his luck was bad, so what? He was used to it by now. If she was gone, if she didn't want him, who would he have to blame but himself? He would just have to take it like a man and move on.)

It is as though he has travelled both backward and forward through time when he pulls into that driveway and steps out of his truck. He steps out of the truck onto that same driveway where he had left them, his boots crunching across the gravel. In the bright sunlight before him are his two grown daughters: one in the distance, her back pressed against the front door; one standing just there, maybe twenty feet in front of him, her hair golden against the vivid turquoise of her truck. One hand on the roof, leaning. One hand on her hip. Darren pans sideways to see, between parted curtains in the front window, a small moon of a face looking out at him. Eyes dark and wide like his one true love. Possibly, this is his granddaughter.

He is weak with it. His faint hope.

BECAUSE FAMILY CAN GET ON YOUR VERY LAST NERVE

Just one minute earlier, Trudy had been filled with heat and rage, ready to burst through the front door and storm over to that truck and what? *What, Trudy? What were you going to do? Hit somebody? Scream and yell and cry like a big baby? And then what?* They would all still be there. Her family. Every single fucking one of them.

It didn't matter what she did. She caught sight of him and her power was gone. It just drained away. Her father, standing there at the end of the driveway. She knows it is him. No question. He looks just like she remembers him, and he looks just like her sister. Her sister who has just jumped down from the truck, who is now swivelling around to take in this interloper. This scene-stealer whose identity is not yet known to her.

Trudy feels her shoulders pulling forward and down toward the ground. She leans back against the door and her knees buckle and bend until she is almost kneeling. As if she is being crushed by an actual physical burden. And just when she thinks it can't get any worse, here she is. *Miss America*. Trudy can see her mother's spun sugar hair and pink lipstick floating above the wheel of her rusty Chevette as she pulls into the driveway.

Behind Darren's truck.

Which is behind Tammy's truck.

Which is right on the very edge of Trudy's last nerve.

BECAUSE CRYING WHEN YOU ARE
HAPPY MAKES NO SENSE TO CHILDREN

Mercy pushes against the screen door with her shoulder, putting all of her weight into it. She can see Trudy on the other side, crouching down.

"Trudy! *Move!*"

Speckles is licking Mercy's face. She lifts her chin and turns her head away from the dog's kisses and pushes harder against the door. Finally, Trudy stands up and staggers out of the way as Mercy and Speckles come tumbling out the door. Mercy regains her composure and walks toward her mother. At least, she thinks it's her mother. There is something about her that puts Mercy off, that doesn't look quite right. She casts a glance at Fenton. She doesn't like the way his leather belt seems to go diagonally across his skinny body and the way he hunches over at the shoulders. And she doesn't think she likes his twitchy face.

Mercy almost can't look at Tammy; she is so beautiful, so confusing. Her hair is so shiny and her eyes are pale and blue. *Wolf eyes*, she thinks. Is this really her mother? Tammy crouches down to Mercy's level, but Mercy holds out a hand, keeping her at bay. She is afraid. Plus, there is something else she needs to do. "Just wait. I'll be right back. I need to talk to Grandma Claire."

Mercy and Speckles continue down the long driveway toward Claire and the man. It looks as if there has been an accident: the driver doors of both vehicles stand open; Claire's car is still running, and a bell sounds from inside. *Ding, ding, ding.* Darren and Claire stand there with their arms at their sides, looking each other up and down, as if checking for injuries. They are crying and laughing at the same time. This makes no sense to Mercy. She doesn't understand why anyone would do this. She has only ever done one thing or the other: laugh or cry. She is never happy and sad at the same time.

"Grandma Claire, what is it?" Speckles is weaving in and out of the feet of the adults, whining. "Are you happy or are you sad?"

Claire thinks that, for once, everything looks beautiful through her tears. Everybody and everything is watery and shining. "Oh, I'm happy, hon. Just a little worn out."

"She cries all the time, you know." Mercy directs this to Darren. "Here." Mercy takes one of Darren's hands and one of Claire's and brings them together as though they are shaking hands. They hold on and squeeze.

"There," says Mercy. "Try that."

BECAUSE SOMETIMES YOU LOSE THE THREAD

Fenton is pretty sure he knows what is happening here. This is the whole family. Claire, Trudy, and Mercy match Tammy's descriptions precisely. And anyone could guess that this other man is Tammy's father. He has her eyes, her smile, her strong chin.

Here we all are, thinks Fenton, *set out in a spray*. It is like a constellation fanning out from the single figure at the doorway of the house (Trudy), connecting to a dot here (Tammy) and there (Fenton), and ending in a tight cluster of three (Darren, Claire, Mercy) at the end of the laneway. And just like a constellation, once you see all of the stars together, once you see that they make a shape, you can almost see a white line connecting them. Standing there in the driveway, Fenton can see a faint white shimmering thread travelling through the air from one person to the next. It disappears in the sunlight if he looks at it head-on, but if he turns his head just slightly away, it's there.

Fenton loses sight of the thread as a cloud slides across the sun. It is colder and darker and trouble is coming. He can feel it.

He walks over to the grass by the driveway and lies down on his back and waits for the feeling to pass.

BECAUSE SOMETIMES YOU FEEL
LIKE A SHEET ON THE CLOTHESLINE

Tammy was not prepared for what faced her when she arrived at her mother's house. She had expected to come back and find Mercy changed, possibly distant, maybe angry with her for leaving. She thought that she could overcome all of that, given a chance. She thought that she could earn her daughter's trust if she stuck around for a while and behaved herself. Tammy had expected Trudy to be angry with her and Claire to welcome her warmly, sloppily, sweetly. With relief and gratitude. She had hoped that Fenton would hold it together, would stand by her. At least for a minute.

But here's what is happening now.

Fenton is lying on the ground on his back, his head turned to the side, his left foot twitching. Mercy is sitting on the ground beside him, smoothing his hair back from his forehead and whispering. The dog, the big fat ungainly dog, is tenderly licking Fenton's hand.

Claire is weeping and holding the hand of the man Tammy supposes is Darren Robertson, the love of Claire's life, the missing link. According to folklore, Tammy's own father.

Trudy is standing at the doorway, stunned, looking like she has been hit in the head with a plank. Frankly, nobody is paying any attention to Tammy at all. She feels like a sheet on the clothesline, waiting for a breeze. Limp. Unmoved.

My daughter looked right through me. She walked right past me.

Mercy, who is five years old, and has no right to have any idea who she is, who has nothing to base an opinion on, saw her, recognized her, and walked right past her. Twice. Once to check on Claire and once to help Fenton. Who she has never even heard of before. Tammy's mother and sister have not seen her in years and they seem not to have noticed her at all. *My arms are empty*, thinks Tammy. Maybe that's how they are supposed to be.

Mercy rests her hand on Fenton's brow and looks over at her mother. Mercy is squinting into the sunlight, but Tammy knows she is looking straight at her. It seems as though she might say something, but then she stops. She changes her mind. Little Mercy stands up and turns toward the house. "Trudy! Something's wrong with my mom's friend!"

BECAUSE YOU DON'T WANT TO HEAR IT

What is Trudy thinking, slumped there against the front door? She is thinking that she doesn't want to hear a word from any of them.

Not from her mother, not from her sister, and not from her so-called father.

Whatever they say will hurt.

None of it will be right and none of it will be enough.

She is thinking that it is much better to be around people you don't care about because they can't hurt you. Not really. Only people you love can tear you apart by just saying the wrong thing. Or not saying the right thing. Or saying the right thing at the wrong time. They can just hurt you by being themselves.

Ugh. *Love.*

And speaking of love, where is Jules? What is the point of him? *What is he for* if he isn't here with her right now? Why does she have to go through this alone?

Speaking of love, who in God's name is that guy with Tammy? He looks like he's been taken apart and put back together wrong. He looks under-done.

And, finally, speaking of love, can her mother's years of stu- pidity really be rewarded so lavishly? Is a dream coming true at the end of the driveway? It is impossible for Trudy to know how to feel about this. Has her father even looked at her?

Because she can't help it, Trudy is also thinking about how everybody else might hurt everybody else. How Darren will hurt Claire and Tammy. How Tammy will hurt Mercy. And how Mercy will hurt Tammy right back.

And because no one else will think about it, she can't help thinking about dinner and sleeping arrangements and about how she will get her car out of the driveway to get to work.

Trudy is thinking all of these things when Mercy calls to her and she looks up to see Tammy's companion collapsed on the lawn like a crumpled up old tissue.

BECAUSE IT'S ALWAYS JUST THE BEGINNING

Trudy ducks into Claire's car and turns off the ignition. Closes the door. She walks over to where Fenton is lying on the ground and stands there, hands on hips. "What's his name, Tammy?"

Mercy says, for no reason, "I think it's Jonathon. He looks like he's named Jonathon."

"Fenton," says Tammy. "His name is Fenton."

"What?" Trudy can't get it. Benson?

Tammy casts her eyes skyward, takes a deep breath, and bellows: "FENTON. HIS NAME IS FENTON!"

At this, Fenton stirs. He rolls onto his side and starts coughing.

"OK, Fenton. Alright. Mercy, take your mom inside and see if you can find something for dinner. We'll be there in a sec." And Mercy walks over to her mother, Speckles in tow, takes her hand without looking up at her face, and pulls her toward the house. "Don't worry. Trudy will take care of Fenton. She knows how."

Claire and Darren have climbed into his truck and are talking, laughing, crying. Lovestruck. Oblivious. Otherwise engaged.

Trudy kneels on the grass beside Fenton. The breeze is cold and fresh. It smells like the river. She looks at this man curled up on the ground and tries to imagine how he fits into her sister's life. As a match, it is implausible. There doesn't seem to be enough of him there to withstand her. He can't weigh more than a hundred and twenty, a hundred and thirty pounds. She is surprised by the tenderness she feels for this stranger, lying there like that on the grass.

"Fenton?" What the hell kind of name is Fenton? "Fenton? Do you think you can get up now?"

"It's almost over," he says. "It's almost over now."

"Oh, I don't think so," says Trudy. "Come on, pal." She pulls him up by both hands. She puts her arm around his skinny waist and jams her shoulder into his armpit to steady him before guiding him toward the house.

BECAUSE THE YEARS COME CHARGING IN

Time has travelled in a circle. Here they are once again. Kissing in a truck. Hiding from the world. Two decades of longing culminating in a deep, long, sigh. A tumbling swoon.

There are wild horses in Claire's chest when he kisses her. Thundering, galloping horses. His hands are in her hair, his cheek is against her cheek, and then he is kissing her and there are horses. He touches her waist, the small of her back, and she feels she will die of it. She will die of the sweetness of the relief of having him in her arms again.

Claire knows what she should do. She knows she should bring him into the house to talk to the girls. She should introduce him to Mercy, his granddaughter. But she can't. She knows she should go see her daughter who has been away for so very long, and even though she is yearning to hold her in her arms and to stroke her hair, she can't do it. Even though she is starting to shiver in the cold cab of the truck, even though the sun is starting to fade in the sky, she can't do it. Her cheek is on his chest and she can hear his heart beat. She can smell his shirt. Her hand is on his hand. His skin is rough and dry and warm. Everything has changed and nothing has changed. Thank God nothing has changed.

She doesn't want to hear a word about what his life has been like without her, what he has been doing all this time. She doesn't want to hear what Trudy thinks or what Tammy thinks. Not yet. She wants to make believe. She wants to make it believable: that he is here, that he has always been here.

Just for a few minutes.

Before everyone starts talking. And all the years come charging in to complicate the story.

BECAUSE LOVE IS WEIRD

Mercy is standing on a kitchen chair at the stove, moving ground beef around a frying pan with a wooden spoon and explaining to Tammy how to make Hamburger Helper. Tammy can see she is warming to her role as hostess. It is as if she is pretending she is on a TV cooking show. Smiling into the camera. She flicks her hair over her shoulder and turns back to Tammy.

"You just keep stirring the hamburger until it is all brown and there is no pink left. Then you add the powder."

"How do you know how to cook, Mercy?" Tammy is fidgeting nervously at the counter beside Mercy, wondering what her role is. She feels like she is failing a test of some kind. Is this right? Were she and Trudy allowed to use the stove when they were — what — five years old? Should she stop the child from cooking? It seems like it would hurt Mercy's feelings if Tammy tried to stop her.

"Grandma Claire taught me. I can make scrambled eggs, too. And soup if it is the canned kind. You can help if you want. Just open that packet and sprinkle the powder around."

Tammy does as she is told. She opens the packet and sprinkles the beige-orange powder over the very cooked hamburger. "Now some water!" Mercy gestures at the cupboard. "Just fill up one of the big coffee cups with warm water and pour it in. When it bubbles, we can add the macaroni. I *love* macaroni." A salty mist rises off the pan as Tammy pours in the cup of water.

"Did you miss me, Mercy?" Tammy is trying to provoke something, to break into the steady stream of cheerful chatter. Why does her child seem like a stranger? She can't find anything in her that seems familiar. Tammy doesn't feel like a mother. She feels tough like gristle.

Mercy looks at the pan and stirs the beef around with the wooden spoon as Tammy pours in more water. "I think so. But it was hard to remember you. You were gone so fast."

Tammy's heart shrinks a little. She puts the coffee cup in the sink.

"I always wished you would come back, though." Tammy can see Mercy is choosing her words. "I just didn't know what it would be like."

"So what's it like?" Tammy regrets asking it. It is too soon. There is nothing good to say yet. Maybe there won't ever be.

"I don't know. Weird. Scary. Crowded." Mercy blows her bangs off her forehead.

"Crowded?" Tammy thinks she knows what she means.

"Yeah. I didn't think there would be so many people all at once."

"Me neither."

"Is Fenton your boyfriend?"

"Uh-huh," says Tammy. "Can you believe it?"

"Not really." Mercy starts giggling, and Tammy is laughing, too. Poor Fenton! They shouldn't be laughing. "He seems nice, though."

Tammy nods, still laughing. And crying a little bit now. "Oh, he is. Fenton is very, very nice. He's just weird."

BECAUSE SOONER OR LATER YOU
HAVE TO MAKE YOUR MOVE

Trudy, Tammy, Mercy, and Fenton are sitting at the table, eating Hamburger Helper. Speckles finishes licking her bowl in the corner of the kitchen and comes over to lay down under Mercy's chair. Mercy puts her bare feet on the dog's back, her toes digging into the soft, warm fur.

Trudy turns to her sister. "I think our mother is having sex in a truck in the driveway."

"Disgusting," says Tammy.

"Probably true, though."

Fenton gets up and clears the plates, walks over to the sink, and runs some water. He froths up the soap with his hands and whistles a little tune.

Tammy shakes her head. "I can't believe it. I sort of felt like he didn't really exist."

"I know." Trudy is pretty sure she doesn't want to be there when Claire and Darren come inside. She's just not up to it. She doesn't want to see their faces, all flushed and happy. And she doesn't want to hear any explanations. Not yet. It always seems to her that the things that most need explaining (like why you left your children, for example) can't really be explained. She hates explanations. They are never good enough.

She still has her mother's car keys in her pocket. Maybe she will just go for a little drive before work.

Maybe she'll drive by Jules's place and see if he is back yet.

But just as she is about to make her move, there they are in the doorway: love's not-so-young dream. Larger than life, standing arm-in-arm, radiating some kind of magic. Making the brown linoleum seem like the gleaming dance floor at the fairy-fucking-princess ball.

Claire walks up behind Tammy's chair and puts her arms around her daughter and nuzzles into her hair, her neck. "My baby is home." Tammy shrugs, closing the gap between jaw and shoulder, squeezing her mother out. Claire is undeterred. She kisses the top of Tammy's head and squeezes her hard.

Tammy turns her face to the side, tears streaming down her face.

Mercy drops to the floor and lays her head down on the dog's soft back.

Trudy gets up from the table, keys in hand. She passes Darren on the way out, gives him a brisk pat on the shoulder as if to say, *You better get in there, pal. This is your moment.*

Darren walks over and squats down beside Mercy and Speckles. "Come on, you two. Let's go for a little walk."

BECAUSE IT WILL ALL END ONE WAY OR ANOTHER

Jules is driving back from Montreal with five hundred dollars in his pocket and the promise of a new investor. Or the ghost of a whisper of a promise. He pulls off the 401 onto winding Highway 2 at Cornwall, just to slow down and take in the sights. And to get his story straight. There will be some explaining to do when he gets back to Preston Mills. He has been gone for ten days. He was supposed to be back in three.

He will tell Trudy about his meetings with Guy, the film producer who might buy the rights to film the jump now that his TV deal is well and truly dead. Guy has mostly produced pornographic shorts for coin-operated peep-show film booths, but those are still films and he has still produced them.

He will not tell Trudy what he did to earn five hundred dollars in ten days. This included: a bare-knuckle fight (which he lost); a bet on a bare-knuckle fight (which he won); a minor drug deal (low-risk, with known participants); and a slightly distasteful sexual favour (better forgotten). Nor will he tell her where he slept (in his car in a parking lot by a warehouse by the river).

He looks like he has been dragged behind a tractor. And he doesn't smell very good, either.

Gliding around curve after curve in the road, the sky soft over the river to his left, Jules is starting to feel just a little bit hopeful. He will go home, take a shower, and go see Trudy and tell her all about his plans.

Jules feels like maybe he is back in charge. He will get his own movie made about the jump — with Guy's help — and he will do his own promotions. He will need new investors to get the ramp and the car into shape. It will take some time. Trudy will like that part, anyway. Surely, she will forgive him the rest. Maybe he will stop and buy her a present. Something for Mercy, too. A belated birthday present. He is thinking of the gift shop near Ingleside where they sell beaded moccasins and snow globes and little silver spoons with tiny ships on the handles. Or maybe that shop is closed for the season now. Never mind. He will come up with something. As he heads out of town past the paper mill, Jules sees the biggest ship he has ever seen. It is blue on the bottom and white on the top and the bow seems to be coming up onto the shore.

He pulls onto the gravel shoulder. There is a crowd of maybe thirty men standing around on the shore, hands in pockets. As Jules approaches, he sees that the ship is still and has run completely aground. It is at a slight angle, almost parallel to the shore, its bow resting in the muddy riverbed. The shallow waves eddy around it gently, making it seem like it is rocking a little, side to side. He is astonished by the height of it, the length, the sheer mass. It towers ten stories high. All spectators are silenced by the strangeness of it. In the middle of the river, a ship looks reasonable, sensibly sized; here on the riverbank, it is as incomprehensible as a flying saucer touching down in the backyard. Nobody expects a ship to heave itself right up onto the muddy earth like that. It looks like it could have kept right on going, across the grassy park and onto the highway.

It looks like the weight of it could split the earth in two.

Jules walks along the grass, along the length of the boat to the stern. There is no sign of life aboard. Where are the men? Below deck? Have they been taken away somewhere already? It is like a ghost ship. Abandoned. He sees the keel, fully exposed, a tangle of seaweed hanging off the top. Something long and slick and black detaches from the knot of weeds, drops into the shallow grey water and slithers away.

And standing there on the shore, Jules lets himself think that one black thought he never allows himself to think. Just for a moment. Then he turns away. Back to the car. Back on track.

Like the man said: *The stunt to end all stunts.*

BECAUSE THEY'RE ONLY NUMBERS

He is crazy. What the hell was he thinking? He had only meant to get something small, just a gesture. A humble apology. But here he is, stumbling into the bright light of the parking lot of the flea market off the highway with a giant teddy bear in his arms and a ring in his pocket and half his money gone already.

Jules had paid five bucks for the teddy bear. It is almost as big as he is and bright pink with a white belly and muzzle. With black glass eyes and a black plastic nose. He had hefted it onto his hip and started down the crowded corridor of the market, trying not to sweep goods off the tables as he passed. He had seen the stand from a long way off, the fat old biker behind the table, his shaggy beard, his hairy belly peeking out of the bottom of a faded black T-shirt. There was an old cracked aquarium sitting there, full of jewelry. Gold chains and plastic beads and silver bracelets and rhinestone earrings piled on top of each other in a tarnished, mouldering mass. *Here*, he thought, *are some deals to be had*. A necklace for Trudy, maybe a little trinket for Mercy.

But no.

That biker had seen him coming with his giant pink bear in his arms. He had seen that look in his eye. The look of the penitent, of a man in the doghouse. Easy prey.

The biker pulled a dark green velvet tray from a box at the back. Twenty, thirty rings in rows. All of them crappy. Dull, bent, pathetic. Stones missing. Except one. (Clever salesman!) One ring in the very middle of the tray. An opal surrounded by rubies set in gold. Gleaming, polished gold. Pink, blue, yellow sparks flashing in that milky stone. From Australia, the man said. Antique, he claimed. A real beauty. A bargain at twice the price.

Jules plucked the ring from the tray and slid it onto his left pinkie finger. He spread his fingers and held his hand out at arm's length. Absurd, this beautiful, delicate thing on his nasty hand. Hairy, with crooked knuckles from bad breaks, and scarred. That first night Trudy had stayed over, she had held his hand in both of hers, running a finger over the perfectly round scars clustered in a pyramid on its back. A game from his youth. What was it? You and your opponent each held a five-dollar bill over the back of your hand, and if you could burn a hole through it with a lit cigarette, you could keep both bills. Or the first person to quit lost, and the other got to keep both bills. Either way, you came out of it scarred for life. He hadn't cared. He had needed the money. And pain could be reassuring sometimes.

"Pretty stupid to do it once," she had said.

"Yeah."

"But three times."

"I know."

She had kissed him then, put his stupid hand on her soft breast.

Jules slipped the ring off his finger. He loved it. He had never seen anything like it. Trudy would love it! His money was there in a thick roll in his front pocket. Burning a hole, as the saying goes. The bristly old biker took the ring back, his fingernails filthy. With a flourish he polished the stone on his shirt and placed it into a ring box shaped like a silver bell and snapped the lid shut. Sold!

Easy come, easy go, thinks Jules as he drives down the highway toward Preston Mills. Money. What does it mean anyway? He swallows hard, thinking of the bills at home, the stalled construction at the ramp site. They're only numbers, he tries to convince himself. Oh, well. It is going to take a lot more than five hundred bucks to get him out of the hole he was digging anyway. It really is a beautiful ring. He looks over at the pink bear in the passenger seat and starts laughing, shaking his head. He pushes his foot down hard on the accelerator just to feel the back of his head press against the headrest. The sun is starting to sink in the sky as he roars down the road, his heart on fire with love and his belly full of dread.

"Doesn't matter! Never mind!" he says out loud.

DOESN'T-MATTER-NEVER-MIND!

Never mind, never mind, never mind.

BECAUSE THERE ARE TWO KINDS OF SURPRISES

Trudy pulls off the gravel road, into Jules's place. She pulls up right to the end of the yard, so the fronds of the weeping willow brush up over the hood. The tree bows in the wind and the branches billow in and out like curtains. Leaves spiral to the ground in a shower of gold and green. On the marshy bank of the bay, white fluff bursts out of the brown velvety cattails. Little brown birds hop from stalk to stalk, wings flickering in the dusky light, heads turning sharply to one side and then the other. In minutes, the sun will be down. Early to come and black as crow feathers, these autumn evenings.

She hears his car on the gravel road before he pulls in behind her. The headlights fill her car, and she tries to fight the lift she feels, the mix of relief and excitement. The craving to see his face, to touch him. She wants to stay angry so she can tell him how lonely she felt when he was gone, how terrible it was to face things without him, how very many things there have been to face. But all of this starts to sound like love, somehow. Like desperation. And she doesn't like it one bit. She straightens up in her seat. Tries to reset her thoughts.

The car smells like her mother's perfume. Which is both comforting and infuriating. Trudy gets out of the car and turns around to face him.

And there he is.

He is standing there holding a giant pink teddy bear. His hair is mashed in on one side and fanned out in a kind of spray on the other. He has a black eye and a fat lip, his shirt is torn, and he has the beginning of a very black beard. He looks like hell. He looks like a drunken pirate. For a second, she isn't sure if it is actually him.

"What the hell happened to you?"

"Oh, Trudy. I really wanted to get cleaned up before I saw you." Jules reaches up and touches his own face, runs his hand over his hair. He bows his head toward his left armpit and recoils. "I'm sorry. Give me a second. Just come in and sit down for a second. I have a surprise for you."

I've had about all the surprises I can take today, thinks Trudy.

She sits at the Formica table, facing the bear seated across from her, and listens to the shower run. She pictures him in there, soaping up, the water streaming over him, and the tight knot that has been in her throat all evening loosens and she starts to weep. Her body shakes and heaves. She pushes her chair back from the table and the bear flops over onto the floor. She climbs the stairs, taking her clothes off as she goes.

Holding him tight, the hot water running over their bodies, she realizes that she doesn't care if her father stays or leaves. She doesn't care if her mother makes a fool of herself. But she does care about one thing. She says it out loud.

"If my sister upsets that child, I will kill her."

BECAUSE SOMETIMES IT SEEMS LIKE THERE IS ONLY ONE KIND OF LUCK

Jules is driving Trudy to work, thinking about the ring in his pocket. Thinking maybe he really will make the jump. Maybe it will all work out after all. Then he'll be rich. Then he could buy Trudy a great big diamond. A little house. Or whatever she wanted. He would just have to hang in there until then. Make his own deals. Secure the financing, fix the ramp, get the job done. Make the jump, let the cash rain down. He would have to hustle, though. In a month, a month and a half, there will be snow, and he can't bear the thought of waiting until next year. But it won't come to that. It will all come together. Jules can feel it.

"What do you think about getting married?" He just says it, throws it out there. Jules looks briefly over at Trudy, then back at the road.

"What do you mean, *what do I think*? About marriage in general?"

"Well, no. You and me. Do you ever think about us getting married?"

"Are you asking me to marry you?" Jules is not sure why this is making her angry, but he can tell it is making her quite angry indeed. His face feels hot.

"Uh, well. I thought we could just talk about it a bit." He really hasn't thought this through. He should have thought it through.

"If this is you asking me to marry you, this is the worst proposal *ever*. What are you doing? Why are you talking about this now?"

"I was just thinking about it."

"So how would it work, Jules? Do we get married before you kill yourself trying to jump over the river? It'd be a short marriage."

"Trudy."

"Or do we just pretend we'll get married after? Good trick. Thanks, Jules. Thanks a lot." He knows that his gestures are falling short. That the only credible way to show her that he loves her would be to shut the whole thing down. Stop plotting and scheming. Admit defeat. But it's too late. Jules hadn't planned for this. He never expected to have something to live for.

Trudy looks out the window as the black trees go by in the black night, lined up along the side of the road. "I can't even talk about this. I hate talking about this."

"Here." Keeping his eyes on the road, Jules pushes the silver bell across the seat, nudges her thigh with it. "Take this. Let's just see what happens. You never know."

Trudy opens the box and looks at the ring. She tries it on a few fingers before slipping it on the middle finger of her left hand. A perfect fit. She looks out the window and flips him the bird with her bejewelled digit. "It's bad luck, you know."

"What is?"

"An opal. Opals are bad luck. Everyone knows that."

"Perfect," he says and smiles out at the night. He looks over at her and, begrudgingly, she is smiling, too. He pushes down hard on the gas, and they fly through the dark toward the lights of the factory.

BECAUSE SOME THINGS JUST DON'T FEEL NATURAL

There is almost always someone sleeping in this house now. Mercy feels like she and Speckles have to be quiet all the time. There is nowhere to go to play. Except outside.

Grandma Claire and Grandpa Dee sleep in the living room. Grandma gets up early like Mercy and Speckles, but Dee sleeps longer, snoring away on the hide-a-bed, hugging the blankets. But not as long as Tammy and Fenton! They stay up late and sleep late. At night, they sit in the kitchen, drinking beer and smoking cigarettes. In the morning, Mercy has to tiptoe out of the bedroom so she doesn't wake them. Fenton sleeps right on the floor beside Tammy's single bed. Like a dog! He doesn't even have a pillow. He just rolls up his jean jacket and puts it under his head.

And Trudy sleeps all afternoon in Mercy's bed. Unless she is with Jules.

It has been a whole week, and Mercy still hasn't touched her mother. And Tammy hasn't touched her. Not like Grandpa Dee. The very first day he was here, he swept Mercy right off her feet and put her on his shoulders. Easy as that. Every time he walks by, he pats her on the head or gives her shoulder a squeeze. Like he loves her just because she is a kid or just because Grandma Claire loves her. Simple.

But Mercy is scared of her mother, and she is not sure why. She has never seen her get angry, but she is afraid of her getting angry. She doesn't act like other adults that Mercy knows. Instead of talking to you, she just gives you warnings. Half the time she doesn't say anything at all, and the other half she just tells you what not to do. Don't ever do this. Don't ever do that. Things you would never think of doing anyway. Mercy thinks that Tammy gives off something electrical, like a spark or a shock that keeps you away. It gives Mercy bad dreams. She keeps dreaming about walking into the living room and seeing a stranger in a chair in the corner. A man with yellow lenses in his glasses and messy hair. Just sitting very still, like a statue or a mannequin. Then Trudy comes in and says, "Mercy, it's your mom!"

She says it so loud it wakes Mercy up every time.

And sometimes she dreams that they are gone. That she wakes up one morning and Tammy and Fenton are gone. She looks out the window at the driveway and the turquoise truck is gone.

Like thieves in the night is what Grandma Claire would say.

Quiet as thieves in the night.

BECAUSE SOME PEOPLE NEVER LEARN

Five adults, one child, and one dog in that tiny house. Four of them sharing a bedroom. *Surprisingly*, Trudy thinks, *it has gone pretty well*. For the first few weeks, anyway. Darren, clearly, is going nowhere. He has already started doing odd jobs around town, employing Fenton when he can. Claire is in top dizzy form, fussing, cleaning, cooking, kissing, and cuddling every person that gets within range. Singing mushy songs all the while.

Speckles likes everybody. Except possibly Trudy. But the feeling is mutual.

Trudy is enjoying the freedom of having more pairs of hands, more volunteers for the school run. And more opportunities to slip out and visit Jules. Because, let's face it, she is in love.

For Mercy, though, things have been mixed. She loves having people around and is especially fond of Darren and Fenton, but at night she has been having bad dreams.

And there is Tammy. *There is always Tammy*, thinks Trudy. No surprises there. Several times, she has seen Mercy come running down the stairs or down the hall, catch sight of Tammy, and stealthily retreat. Similarly, Tammy seems to leave every room Darren enters.

Less subtle is the Tammy and Fenton dynamic. Tammy is routinely cruel to Fenton, calling him names and mocking him, but last week Trudy saw a few things that she really wishes she hadn't seen.

It was a sunny day, and Trudy was sitting on a lawn chair in the yard, watching Fenton play Frisbee with Mercy. Speckles was tracking the orange disc as it sailed through the air, shuffling halfheartedly after it, one way and then the other. Mercy's throws were mostly wild and off-course, and Fenton gamely retrieved and returned each one.

"FENTON!" Tammy was suddenly on the front step, eyes shooting daggers at the happy scene before her. "Let's go!"

Fenton, to Trudy's astonishment, ignored Tammy and went jogging off to retrieve the Frisbee from the driveway. He sent it back toward Mercy, smiling at her. "We're just going to finish our game, right Mercy?"

"Right," said Mercy and sent another one sailing high over Fenton's head. Fenton jogged away again and bent to pick up the Frisbee, but as he turned to throw it back, he was confronted with a furious Tammy standing right before him. She had actually jumped off the step and raced across the yard. She grabbed the Frisbee and threw it on the ground.

"STOP!" cried Mercy, as her mother shoved Fenton with both hands flat against his chest. He stumbled back a few steps. Tammy picked up the Frisbee and started hitting him over the head with it. Fenton raised his arms, crossing his wrists in front of his face in surrender. Trudy was out of her chair and heading across the yard.

"Are you somebody's daddy now, Fenton? Is that what you think you are?" Tammy threw the Frisbee on the ground in disgust and stormed back to the house, almost knocking Trudy over as she passed. "And fuck you, too, Trudy."

Fenton smiled weakly, patting the weeping Mercy on the head, and followed Tammy into the house to make amends.

And then, a couple days later, Trudy had witnessed something else.

She had been driving home from the grocery store when she had seen them. There, standing outside the pool hall was her sister, tits almost spilling out of her too-tight top, head thrown back in laughter, her lipsticked mouth open wide. And beside her, head down, sly smirk on his face, was that weasel, Sammy Harrison. As Trudy drove by, Sammy reached out and pulled Tammy close, cupping her ass in both hands.

That's more like it, thought Trudy. *They deserve each other, those two.*

And, finally, a couple days after that, Trudy saw Fenton and Tammy sitting in the truck in the driveway, fighting, crying, and then falling into each other's arms.

Dear God in heaven. It was sad but true: some people never, ever learn.

BECAUSE IT HAS ALWAYS BEEN SERIOUS

"So this Jules guy."

"Yeah?" It is late morning and Tammy and Trudy are drinking coffee in a booth at the Jubilee. Fenton has been sent on an errand of some kind.

"Your boyfriend."

"Uh-huh."

"Is he French or something?"

"Yes, Tammy. He's French."

"Thought so. He looks like fucking Blacque Jacques Shellacque or something." Tammy laughs at her own joke, puts another cream in her coffee. "Honestly."

"Hilarious."

"Don't get touchy. I was just asking. He's just got that lumberjack look, you know? All eyebrows and curly hair." She looks at Trudy dead-on, now. Trying to read her. "You think he'll really make that jump?"

"I don't know. Maybe?" Trudy would rather not go down this road with her sister this morning. She wishes they had something to talk about that didn't matter. But it has never been that way between them. It has always been serious. Hard going. Love and hate, sound and fury.

Tammy takes a drag from her cigarette and blows the smoke up over Trudy's head. She sounds bored. "It's pretty far. And that ramp doesn't look right. Fenton and I drove out there yesterday, and it looks like it's about to fall over." *There is something weird about Tammy now*, thinks Trudy. Something new and hard. Robotic. It's like she doesn't know she is talking to a human being about another human being. A person she loves. Who might die.

"Can we change the subject? Why don't we talk about your daughter, for example?"

"Right." Tammy drums the tabletop with her thumbs. "Seems more like your daughter, if you ask me."

The hair on the back of Trudy's neck stands up, and her scalp tingles. She is not sure she can have this conversation, either. Not in any civilized way. "What's going on, Tammy? Are you mad at me for taking care of your daughter for you all this time? If so," she makes a sweeping gesture with her arm like she is taking a bow, "then *fuck you*."

"Yeah, fuck me. I'm terrible and you're great." Tammy fakes a smile with her teeth.

But her eyes are dead.

THE STUNT

BECAUSE MAYBE THEY REALLY ARE TRYING TO KILL YOU

Jules puts the phone down. Defeated again. Guy is out. No deal. The bottom, the barrel, scraped clean. He had been kidding himself, as usual.

It would be funny if it weren't so fucking tragic. His cherished rocket-car replica, his star prop for all these years, now mutilated by the angry townsfolk and abandoned in the waving tall grass of the backyard. Orange, yellow, red leaves scattered across the dented hood, fluttering down from above. The JULES TREMBLAY HEADQUARTERS sign bashed in and hanging from one corner on the post by the road. The giant leaning ramp and the ever-diminishing hope of an investor. The rain, rain, rain, endless rain.

The stuntman with the limp and his fading yellow shiner.

But wait! There's more!

How about the cowboy who landed on his head? *Hilarious!*

James and Mark have been and gone weeks earlier, the room cleared out. Boots and all. They moved back to Montreal — recovering from their so-called careers in rodeo. James is looking for a job while caring for Mark, who wears a halo of steel around his head and a cast covering his whole torso. Like some kid's bad space-robot Halloween costume.

They are officially done with The Stupid Life. Jules can well understand it.

It has been raining again for the last month, and Jules wears his winter coat inside the big, empty, rambling house. He will not turn on the heat. There isn't enough money for that. If he is still here — in this town, in this physical mortal realm — when the snow falls, he will see about turning on the heat then. For now, he walks around wrapped in a rainbow-coloured granny-square afghan that Claire crocheted for him. He wears it over his coat to keep out the damp cool air. Occasionally, he even wears a toque. This is the state he is in when Sammy knocks on the door: cold and alone. Despairing of his future, hiding from the world.

The Mad Canadian, indeed.

He flinches when he hears the knock at the door. He considers not answering, just laying low until his visitor gives up.

The knocking comes again in shave-and-a-haircut style. Thump-thumpity-thump-thump. *Thump, thump*. Two bits. So corny. So *showbiz*. It can only be Sammy. Why now? Where has he been all this time while everything was going to hell? Not taking Jules's calls, that's for sure.

Jules shuffles toward the door, not even bothering to take off the afghan. He can't bear the cold. Fuck Sammy if he doesn't like it.

"Hey, Jules. Nice getup." Sammy walks past him and sits at the kitchen table. His jeans are so tight, he doesn't actually bend at the hips. He just catches the edge of the chair with the slight curve of his ass and leans against it like a plank. Cowboy boots straight out in front, crossed at the ankles.

"Got a beer or something?"

"No," Jules lies. "What's up, Sammy?"

"We're gonna do it, Jules. We're gonna do the jump."

"What are you talking about?" *What do you mean we*, he thinks.

"The network called me. They're back in. We're gonna do it two weeks from Tuesday."

Jules can't make sense of this. "Sammy, the ramp is fucked. The car isn't ready. How can we even sell tickets by then?"

"Not selling tickets."

"What do you mean we're not selling tickets?"

"The network doesn't want to sell tickets. Liability or something. They just want to shoot it and get it done."

They're trying to kill me, thinks Jules. "Are they trying to kill me?"

"Relax," says Sammy. "Everything will be fine. Your dream is finally coming true, man! Cheer up!" Sammy gets up from the table and runs a hand through his feathery hair. "Gotta go. Listen: they want to see you in Ottawa on Monday. I'll let you know when I know more. Hang in there, buddy."

He thumps Jules on the back and walks out the door.

Jules is still staring after him when a spider with a body the size and colour of a malt ball drops from the ceiling and dangles in front of his face. He actually squeals and jumps back, pulling his blanket around his shoulders.

BECAUSE YOU DON'T HAVE TO SEE
PEOPLE GO TO KNOW THEY ARE GONE

Trudy can't believe he is going away again. It seems like everybody in the whole world can just come and go as they please, and
she has to stay in Preston Mills and sew pillowcases. What is she
doing wrong?

"I don't know why they want to see me, Trudy. Sammy says the
network wants to renegotiate. Maybe set a new date for the jump."
He is not going to tell her what date they have in mind. Not until
he knows for sure.

"Stupid jump."

"I won't be gone long."

"I've heard that one before." They are sitting in his car in her
driveway. His gym bag is packed and sitting on the back seat. She
doesn't want to get out and watch him drive away. She doesn't
want to hear any more about the jump. It'll never happen anyway,
she is sure of it. Nobody could possibly believe that car could fly.
And the ramp is ridiculous. It all seems like a morbid joke now.
"Don't go. Let's just go somewhere else. Let's just go get Mercy
from school and run away."

He smiles over at her. She is stalling and he knows it. "Yeah?
Where?"

"Anywhere."

"And how would we live? Do they have factories and rocket cars there?"

"They have those everywhere."

"Really?"

"No, not really. They have rocket cars everywhere. Factories are harder to come by. We could try something new. Circus? Freak show? Mercy's small and you're crazy. That must be worth something."

"Get out of my car, lady."

Trudy leans over and gives him a deafening smack of a kiss on his right ear. "If you're not back on Wednesday, I will never forgive you. Don't put me through that again."

"I won't."

She gets out of the car, heads for the house, goes inside.

She doesn't need to see him go to know he is gone.

BECAUSE SOMETIMES YOU CAN SMELL A RAT

Another day, another dollar, thinks Darren as he cleans his brush in the laundry sink. He has repainted the entire ground floor of this big house by the river in less than a week, and he feels good. Fenton couldn't make it again today but that was OK — Darren managed to finish the job by himself. He is whistling to himself, getting ready to leave, when Joe Davis knocks on the door. He says he is selling tickets for the rocket car jump across the river. He lives just across the road from the ramp. (Darren knows this — Davis lives in a trailer so crooked and parked so close to the bank of the river it looks like it might topple in.) He says people are buying tickets to sit in his yard and watch the jump tomorrow.

"Twenty-five bucks each." Davis holds a limp fan of hand-written tickets in his filthy hand. They say: Rocket Car — Admit One — $25. He smells like urine and sweat. Darren looks from the stubbled face down to Joe's mud-covered rubber boots and thanks God he didn't invite him in.

"What are you talking about? Who says the jump is tomorrow?"

"They brought the car up from the States last week. I seen it. They're keeping it at Danny Franklin's garage in Chesterville."

"Listen, I know the guy. He isn't even in town right now. They haven't even finished fixing the ramp."

"Guess he's comin' back then, and I guess it'll have to be done. One o'clock tomorrow is what Danny says. You want some tickets or what? I only got ten left." Darren finds this hard to believe. He finds all of it hard to believe.

"OK, even if the jump was happening, why in the hell would anyone buy tickets? If it was actually happening — which it isn't — and I really wanted to see it, why wouldn't I just drive over there, pull over to the side of the road, and watch it? For free?"

"Suit yourself. Won't be no refreshments, though. Me and the boys are gonna be selling beer, too."

This makes even less sense. Darren thinks about exploring this further — *Why couldn't he bring his own beer?* — but decides against it. There is no point.

"Thanks, anyway." He takes a step backward, reaches for the door.

"You sure? Last chance."

Darren is pretty sure. He raises a hand as if to wave and takes another step back, closes the door. Unbelievable. Darren might be new in town, but he has heard all about this Davis character. He is a known lunatic. Claire told him that Davis used to chase girls when she was a teenager. Just break out and chase them down the street with his dirty hair sticking out all over the place. He never caught Claire, but she heard from other girls that he would knock them to the ground, pin their arms down with his knees, and tickle them. Hard. Then he would just get up and walk away. Leaving them there on the ground.

You might think this would diminish his popularity. But everyone just sort of takes Davis's behaviour as a fact of life. Still wave at him at the gas station or the grocery store, still ask about his family. And they make damn sure they warn their daughters not to walk by his place, to take the long way home if they have to.

Darren has seen some rough towns in his life with some strange people, but Preston Mills is something else.

BECAUSE YOU MADE IT THIS WAY

That night over dinner, Darren tells the story of crazy Joe Davis and his homemade tickets. In the telling, Davis's hair is crazier, his hands dirtier. The tickets are more ridiculous, written in pencil crayon, each the size of a placemat. Mercy laughs. Claire tells Joe Davis stories from her girlhood. Trudy doesn't find any of it very funny. When she and Tammy were girls, they had been terrified of Joe Davis. His catcalls and lewd gestures. His crazy teeth.

And the idea of the jump being real, something that could really happen, is chilling. The thought of Davis and a bunch of drunken fools sitting outside his ruin of a trailer watching it — as though it were *entertainment* — was sickening to her. But of course it is bullshit. It isn't happening. Jules would have told her. He would.

She will call him tonight anyway. Just to make sure.

Trudy wants to enjoy dinner, to savour this harmony. She likes Darren, after all, and she is glad to see Claire and Mercy happy. Tammy and Fenton are eating take-out burgers in the truck, like the weirdos they are — determined to be on the wrong side of everything. Since the Frisbee incident, they have been keeping their distance, and to Darren's irritation, Fenton has been showing up late for work or not at all. *Good*, thinks Trudy. *Stay out there. Don't show up.*

It is better without you.

That's the way you have made it and that's the way it will be.

BECAUSE SOME PEOPLE ARE
HARDER TO LOVE THAN OTHERS

And the next morning, Tammy and Fenton are gone. Just like in Mercy's dream, she wakes up and looks over at the bed across the room, and it is empty. No Tammy curled up in a ball under the blankets, no Fenton on the floor. Mercy is alone. Not sure if she is awake or not, she does what she did in her dream. She pulls the covers back and gets out of bed. She walks across the room to the window and looks out at the driveway. The sun is just rising. It is mostly dark but orange-pink light is beginning to spread across the ground. Claire's car and Darren's truck, the grass in the yard, the stones in the driveway, are all shining in the morning light.

But Tammy's truck is gone.

Mercy puts on her slippers and goes downstairs. The house is quiet and still. There is light coming from the kitchen. Dee and Speckles are asleep on the hide-a-bed, so she creeps by quietly to join Claire who is already up, making toast. She doesn't know if her grandmother knows yet that Tammy is gone and she doesn't want to tell her.

Mercy knows she will be sad. And mad.

She walks over and stands beside her grandmother at the counter and leans against her. Claire reaches down and rests her hand on top of Mercy's head, smooths down her tangled hair. Then she pops up the toast and scrapes some butter on it. "Oh, Mercy," she says. "Just you and me this morning, I guess. Let's make some hot chocolate."

Mercy can't believe this. She never gets hot chocolate during the week. She feels a hundred confusing things at once. She thinks she might cry. "Grandma Claire, I love you."

"I love you, too."

"I'm not sure if I love my mom." She feels terrible for saying it. It is a terrible thing to say, a terrible way to feel.

"Maybe you do."

"I didn't really have time." And now Mercy is crying. She had her chance and she missed it. Her grandmother picks her up like she is a baby, like she weighs nothing at all. Mercy lays her head on Claire's shoulder, lets her stroke her hair and kiss her cheek.

Claire sighs. "She's not easy to love, Mercy."

BECAUSE IT HAS ALREADY HAPPENED WITHOUT YOU

Trudy rarely drinks on workdays, but on the way to pick up Mercy from school, she stops at the beer store and picks up a six-pack. Jules is not returning her calls, and Tammy's sudden departure has shaken Mercy. She is either hyper and crazy or sad and clingy. Trudy's nerves are shot.

After feeding Mercy lunch, Trudy gets the shoebox full of Barbie dolls and clothes and puts it on the kitchen table, hoping she will play quietly for a while, but Mercy is wound up. She wants to play Jungle. Jungle, a game she plays at school with her new friends, is all she wants to play lately. It involves a lot of growling and running around on Mercy's part and some hiding and dying on Trudy's. But Trudy is not in the mood. She takes the lid off the shoebox and heads to the fridge to get a beer. Mercy, disappointed, flops down at the table and starts picking through the tiny dresses. Trudy quietly takes her leave, down the hall, around the corner into the living room. She sits just out of Mercy's sightline.

She has not even taken a sip when the phone rings.

"Trudy?" Before she even says hello, someone is talking. "Trudy, it's Darren. You better get down here." Down where?

Mercy jumps around the corner and raises her two hands high above her head, making claws with her fingers. *"RAHR! GRRRR!"*

Trudy can't hear what he is saying. Now Mercy is standing on the couch, roaring at the top of her lungs, and jumping on the cushions.

"Mercy, for the love of God. Please shut up. Just for a minute."

"I will KILL you!"

"Honey, you won't. Now please be quiet."

"Yes I *will*. I will kill you and EAT YOU!" She leaps off the couch at Trudy and crash-lands in her lap, knocking the beer out of her hand. The bottle hits the wall. Beer sprays everywhere. Mercy takes off. Trudy leaps out of her chair, the phone still pressed against her ear, and glares after Mercy, who is racing up the stairs. She stops mid-flight, curls her hands into claws again, and growls in Trudy's direction, "*RAAHR!*"

"Sorry, Darren. Just a sec." Trudy drops the phone, leaves it dangling from its cord, and runs to the bottom of the stairs. Hopping on one foot, she removes a slipper and pitches it as hard as she can up the stairs at Mercy, who is peering down at her from the top. The slipper bounces off a step and flops end over end back down to the bottom. Trudy picks it up, puts it on, and walks back over to the phone.

"Hi. Sorry. You were saying?"

"You better get down here, Trudy. To the ramp. I was driving back from town and it had already happened. The car is in the water. You better come."

BECAUSE THE WIND MAKES YOUR EYES WATER

Mercy freezes at the top of the stairs. The air is strange. Something is wrong. Trudy makes a noise Mercy has never heard before. Like a dog whining.

It is quiet again for a minute and then, in a new, flat voice, Trudy says, "I'll be there. I'm coming. OK."

Mercy hears the thud of Trudy's footsteps down the hall, the jingle of keys, the back door slamming shut.

"*Hey!*" She is frightened now. She can't be in the house alone. "Trudy!"

No response.

"Trudy! You're not allowed to leave me alone!"

Mercy hears the car starting in the driveway and she runs as fast as she can down the stairs, down the hall, and out the door, into the laneway. The car is idling, Trudy at the wheel, the passenger door hanging open. Mercy stands and stares for a second, her heart pounding. Trudy leans on the horn and Mercy runs to the car, scrambling into the passenger seat. She can barely get the heavy door closed before Trudy is backing out of the driveway and onto the street.

"Fuck!" Trudy says. She says it like she will never stop saying it. "Fuck, fuck, fuck, fuck."

Trudy's hands are shaking as she lights a cigarette with the car lighter and pushes on the gas pedal until it is flat against the floor. Mercy sticks her head out the window into the cold wind. Her hair is flying everywhere, getting in her eyes. It makes them water. The wind on her face blows her tears back toward her ears.

Trudy tells Mercy to get her head back in the car and sit down.

BECAUSE YOU WOULDN'T

Darren hadn't believed Joe Davis for a second. Why not? Because you wouldn't, that's why. The guy was nuts. A madman who chased young girls and tickled them. Who may have never had a bath in his entire life. But here it all was. The whole sad mess.

Darren had spent the morning tearing down an old carport in Morrisburg, feeling every bit his age but enjoying the work. On his lunch break, he thought he would drive down to the locks in Iroquois. He could park the truck and, if his timing was good, watch a boat go through while he ate his lunch. A workman's lunch in a steel lunch bucket: ham sandwiches, two apples, milky tea in a thermos.

He had been heading down Lakeshore Drive, taking the corners nice and easy when he saw a tiny flash of yellow in the grey sky: the car. He was sure of it. Darren stopped the truck right there in the middle of the road and leaned forward, straining to see. It was over in a second. So high in the sky like a pale yellow kite, then a sharp descent, the hood angling sharply down, then dropping out of sight. *Christ*, thought Darren. From where he was sitting, it didn't even look like the car had made it to the water's edge. Just straight up, then straight down. Like an upside-down V.

He put the truck back in gear and slowly made his way toward the site, about a half a mile away. The first thing he saw was a cop car parked across both lanes of the road. Then a crowd of about fifteen men standing around in Joe Davis's yard, looking out over the water. He pulled over and walked across the street to the shore and looked out over the water. There was no car in sight. Just grey, rippling waves. The wind was strong now, blowing his pants against his legs, making him shiver in his sweaty work clothes. He looked back at the ramp. There was a piece of asphalt hanging off the front edge, dangling a hundred feet up. It detached and fell, sending up a spray of muddy gravel when it hit with a thud that shook the ground.

Darren walked over to Joe Davis, that smelly, callous old bastard, and asked to use his phone. He didn't look at any of the "ticket holders." He didn't want to know who they were.

BECAUSE YOU DON'T EVEN KNOW
WHO TO BE MAD AT FOR WHAT

They had met Jules in the lobby when he arrived, three of them. At the Lord Elgin Hotel in Ottawa. The beautiful lobby. There he was in his old jeans and mackinaw, black grease under his fingernails, and the three of them came straight at him, all white shirts and suit jackets and striped ties. And identical curly hair. At least Jules had that part right.

Where was Sammy? Wasn't Sammy supposed to be here?

They took away his gym bag and gave it to a porter. And they steered him straight into the bar where he drank beer and ate nuts until he thought he would explode, listening to their incomprehensible banter. Jules started to think that they didn't seem very believable as American network types. So big and burly. Every time he asked about the jump, they deflected. It wasn't their area, they didn't really work for the network directly, they were contractors. There was no need to worry about that now, he should enjoy himself! A meeting would be set up sometime tomorrow with the lawyers, the programming people, the insurance people. Jules couldn't keep track, the plan changed so many times even over the course of an hour.

They shunted him off to his room and told him to order whatever he wanted from room service. Take it easy. They would be in touch.

That was three days ago. He was supposed to be home yesterday. And for the third day in a row, one of those assholes knocked on his door and told him the meeting had been delayed. There was always a vague reason: scheduling conflicts, flight times, just the crazy ups and downs of the entertainment industry!

Trudy would kill him.

And he thought he would go crazy with boredom: no money to go out — it was pouring rain anyway — and the TV in his room got only a few channels. Out of desperation, he turned it on anyway.

And he just caught it: the grainy footage of something pale yellow against a dark grey sky, and the announcer saying his name, *Daredevil, Jules Tremblay*. He jumped up to turn up the volume, but it was over. On to the next item. Frantically, he switched from channel to channel, hoping to find out more, but the news was over. He sat on the end of the bed and burst into tears.

Fuckers! What had they done?

BECAUSE IT IS JUST A BODY IN THE END

Trudy sees the cars first. So many cars parked by the side of the road. There must be a dozen, all pulled over onto the gravel shoulder of the road. The ramp looks like it's been hit by a meteor. A cop car is blocking traffic. Someone has put a sawhorse beside it. She can see Darren's truck on the other side. "Close your eyes, Mercy."

"Why?"

"Just close them until I tell you to open them." Trudy slows down. There is an ambulance and a firetruck, and she can see Dr. Cameron's car parked in Joe Davis's yard. A white van with an Ottawa TV station logo on the side. She looks out across the water and sees the divers in wetsuits in the boat. A tiny boat with an outboard motor. Whose boat is it? Who are the divers? Trudy can't think straight. She shouldn't have brought Mercy here. She opens the door and gets out. "Stay here, Mercy. Lock the doors."

"Trudy, don't leave me!"

"I want you to lock the doors and lie down on the seat and close your eyes, Mercy."

Mercy is whimpering, whining, no, no, no, but even as she says it she does as she is told: she locks the doors one by one and lies down on the front seat. She hugs her knees to her chest and closes her eyes.

Trudy starts to walk toward the shore but stops. She braces her hands against her knees and vomits onto the grass. She starts to cough and throws up again. *That's alright*, she thinks. *That's fine*. As if anything could possibly be fine. She straightens up and scans the crowd on the grass for Darren, but she can't see him. Then she realizes he is in his truck. She can see him through the windshield, his head on his arms on the steering wheel. The small crowd of people is quiet as she walks by, staring after her. She doesn't look at them. She opens the door of the truck and tells Darren to take Mercy home in her car. She will bring the truck home when she can.

"Will you be alright?"

"No. Never." She says it with dead certainty. She will never be alright again. But she wants him to go and take Mercy with him. They trade keys and she walks back toward the shore. She sits on a cold rock and watches the divers tumble off the boat into the cold grey water.

Darren unlocks the door and starts the engine. He tucks Mercy tight against his side and drives away.

It is not a person. It is a body.

They lean down over the side of the boat and haul the body in. Trudy sees something bloody in the tangle of blond hair before she turns away. The sound carries across the water, the hollow sound of the weight hitting the side, the bottom of the aluminum boat. The splash and drip of water on the hull.

The diver is breathing heavily when he says it. He has to stop and catch his breath. "I'm going back down. There's another one down there. There's someone else."

BECAUSE THERE ARE NO DIAMONDS

The river didn't look like diamonds on that day in November. The stone-grey sky hung above the tips of the white caps, a velvet curtain with lacy trim brushing against the stage. The water churned. Where it was dark it was almost black. And where it was light on the crests of the waves it was a foamy pale grey. Fronds of mossy weed surfaced here and there. Tentacles breaking the surface.

Of course he had offered to drive, but as usual she wouldn't let him. Maybe she didn't believe that he would do it. Maybe she thought he didn't have it in him. But he did. He would. He wasn't afraid. So he would go with her. They were in it together.

She started the car and it rumbled and trembled and sputtered. From the bottom of the ramp, they could only see sky past the end. The clouds rolled like smoke, like spirits. The air was heavy and damp and cold. The asphalt blackened in the shadows.

She pushed the accelerator down to the floor and it roared like thunder. Roared like a lion. King of the jungle. She looked over at Fenton and grinned. They didn't wear helmets. They wanted to see everything.

Fenton had a cigarette dangling from his bottom lip. It almost fell into his lap when she stepped on the gas and hit the rocket booster button. One, two. No messing around. His head hit the headrest and his back was pushed into the seat. He could barely breathe. She was laughing. He was laughing. They held hands as the Lincoln sped up the ramp and the world dropped away. Up, up. The car tilted slightly starboard and the hood kept rising, butter yellow filling their vision.

And then the whole car seemed to tip backward. Suddenly they were hanging from their seat belts, but still rising. Were they upside down now?

Everything outside the car was just grey. Water? Sky? Which way was down?

Orange flames filled the windshield. And then something inky black spread across the glass from the bottom up.

The water hit the roof first, making a hollow sound, then it filled the frames of the windows, black and grey and mossy-green.

It was quiet and muffled.

They could hear each other breathing.

And then they couldn't hear anything at all.

ACKNOWLEDGEMENTS AND THANKS

This book was inspired, in part, by the Mile Jump of Ken Carter, the Mad Canadian. This sad story is beautifully told in Robert Fortier's 1981 NFB film, *The Devil at Your Heels*. I could not have written this book the way I did without having watched it many, many times.

Thank you to my family (especially Peter Shmelzer) for encouragement. Thank you, Andrew Steinmetz, for your help. Thanks to the Banff Centre for peace and quiet. Thank you, Susan Renouf of ECW, for your investment in this story and your skilled guidance. And thank you, Laura Pastore, for your attention to detail.

Finally, I would like to thank Michael V. Smith, who was gracious and kind (and even helpful) when I told him I had written a book with the same title as his excellent collection of poems. Michael: you are a nice person.

MISSY MARSTON's first novel, *The Love Monster*, was the winner of the 2013 Ottawa Book Award, a finalist for the CBC Bookie Awards and the Scotiabank Giller Prize Readers' Choice. She lives in Ottawa, Ontario.